# CRUEL NIGHTS

# ALSO BY JASON NAHRUNG

Blood and Dust

The Big Smoke

Salvage

The Darkness Within

# CRUEL NIGHTS

## JASON NAHRUNG

Brain Jar Press
PO Box 6687
Upper Mt Gravatt, QLD, 4122
Australia
www.BrainJarPress.com



Cover design by Brain Jar Press
Cover Image: Female model in halloween outfit, Gerain0812/Shutterstock

ISBN: 978-1-922479-66-2 (paperback) | 978-1-922479-67-9 (Ebook)

# PRELUDE

## 1973: NEVADA

Charlie died in Shithole, Nevada, a fly speck on Route 93. It was 18 July 1973; he knows this because he still had the ticket from the Led Zep gig in Seattle the night before, the reason he found himself marooned in an even smaller shithole with nothing but a gas station and a T-junction to show for itself.

He can't even tell you the name of the place now, strange as it seems, just that his radiator had given up the ghost and his engine cooked. The gas station he walked to didn't have any parts but did have Coke in the fridge. The attendant and his missus who ran the place, both as weathered as the desert he'd trudged through, were nice enough, talking about putting him up until the next day when they could see about a new engine or give him a tow into town, whatever suited him best.

The memory of the gig was fading like desert haze as he considered the few bucks and last joint in his wallet while he thought about having to tell the boss he'd be missing another day of work, let alone the roasting from his folks, probably a whooping from his pa. A mechanic with a broken-down car in the middle of nowhere and not a radiator hose to save himself.

He was saved, or so he thought, by the Chevy that pulled up just as the owners were turning off the lights for the night.

I'll give you a lift, sure I will, the stranger said, a grin full of teeth, dark hair slicked back, his accent a nowhere thing as the old dude pumped gas into his tank.

Not much a one for conversation, content to twiddle the dial through the scratchy stations, tarmac vanishing in the headlights as though they weren't moving, the engine growl a lie like some kind of show ride, stars blazing out the window moving hardly at all. Charlie asking to turn up the heat, because the driver didn't feel the cold, so he said. Roy, from nowhere in particular, just driving, south when pressed, and the volume turned up then, no more questions. That was when Charlie felt the flip-flop in his gut, but hey, the guy was scrawny, tall, dark in a wop type of way, well manicured. What was the worst he could do?

A couple hours later, he found out.

I gotta stop soon, the driver said. There'll do.

He pointed through his bug-starred windshield at the glow of a town on the horizon. A sign flashed by, missed it, population not many.

I can drive, Charlie said, thinking, it's only three hours to home and the garage. Gonna cost to get the car [he never did].

Sorry, one-man car this. That smile, pale as moonlight.

Well, maybe I can hitch from there.

At least have a coffee and something to eat before you hit the road. A shower, mebbe?

Shoulda listened to that flip-flop, the cold knife of wariness in his gut. But coffee and eggs and a shower after that long drive on Monday night and a fitful sleep in the back seat before the gig, the tobacco and weed and Jim Beam still oozing from his pores.

Sure.

And then it was hands and teeth, and waking up in a bath tub with a foul taste in his mouth. And the world was … changed.

But as Roy told him, the world was no different. It was Charlie who had changed, and there was no going back.

# IN WALKS THE NIGHT



Corey, with piercings in ears and nose, and her purple hair and ripped jeans and leather jacket and Mudhoney t-shirt, was dodging the latest asshole of several assholes, this one a Dire Straits fan judging by his tee. He'd got her in and that's all she'd wanted, slipping away easily in the club seething in a fug of cigarette smoke, sweat and beer. TAD was tearing the place a new one, pogoing fans frothing against the stage, and it was worth the inconvenience of playing nice and that long trolley trip in from neighbouring Renton.

She was pissed at Ruby for being a suck and not coming out; she missed her wingman, but she recognised a couple of faces up the back, nodding along to the aural assault as a fan staggered along the stage in front of the band before hurling himself backwards into the pit.

Oh, shit. One of the jocks up the back was Victor. He'd been buzzing around ever since she'd passed out at his Halloween party last year. For a moment, she wondered if Ruby had planned this. Why else would Police-loving Victor Moreno be here if it wasn't to score brownie points? She ducked away, desperate to avoid eye contact, unsure if he'd seen her. Great, now she had two squares to dodge and still try to have fun tonight.

And there was that short-back-and-sides in the flared jeans and Led Zep tee under a denim jacket somehow alone at the bar that was otherwise three deep, staring into a full glass of beer as though it held some secret. Weedy but … dark, somehow. Her bad news radar pinged loud, louder than the kick drum, louder than it had with the wannabe cruiser who'd been her ticket in, louder then Jimmy who'd given her the split lip and Rob who'd bragged to the entire team. Victor, by contrast, wasn't that bad.

She shouldered up to the dude at the bar and shouted close to his ear, 'Wotcha looking at?'

He eyed her sideways, ridiculously still in the throbbing, smoke-filled room, one eyebrow raised. Such fine cheek bones and barely there eyebrows, and those lips. Eyes the blue of a malamute, staring straight into her. She overcame the sudden catch of her breath.

'Band's thataway.' She jerked a thumb over her shoulder.

'I can hear them just fine,' he said, and almost smiled as though reining in some private joke.

Her gut lurched. Run away, it said. Even the douchebag she'd just ditched was a safer bet.

She leaned in, arm touching his where he cradled the untouched beer. 'You gonna drink that?'

He pushed it across to her.

A thump against her shoulder sent the glass skittling across the bar, a wake of liquid spilling behind it. She whirled around, ready to insist the klutz buy her a new one, and groaned.

'There you are,' the bozo in the Dire Straits tee said.

She crossed her arms. 'You've mistaken me for someone else.'

'In that case, you owe me three bucks for getting you in. Or you want me to tell the management how old you are?'

'How old are you?' the lonely drinker asked, as though the douche didn't exist.

Corey ignored Contemplative Man, her attention on the hassle. 'Just push off.'

He stepped up and she retreated, the hard edge of the bar pressing against her spine.

'She with you?' he asked Mr Contemplative, who shrugged and then pointed to his spilled beer being mopped up by the scowling bar tender.

'Yes,' she said. 'We're married.'

The douchebag laughed. 'Let's talk to the manager, hey.' He gripped her elbow tightly as he steered her roughly through the crowd to the exit past the restrooms.

'The office is thataway,' she said, nodding to a door just glimpsable down a hall.

The douchebag laughed again.

The stench of stale water, rot, piss hit her nostrils as they reached the stairs, just four or so from a narrow loading dock. His grip loosened as she jumped down, dragging him off balance. She got lucky; he slipped, went down on one knee. Her elbow took him in the face, her high-top in the guts. Her toes protested at the impact and she wished she'd been wearing her Docs, but he was holding his gushing nose, swearing incoherently between gasps, so she figured she was in front.

Mr Contemplative stood at the top of the stairs. 'Wanna ride?'

'Thought you'd never ask.'

His car was a big old clunker, dented and rusted with small wings at the back and white-wall tyres, and she was kind of surprised it even started, but it purred along all right once it had cleared its throat. She was just getting used to the mustiness that reminded her of rotted carpet that filled the gap between them on the scuffed bench seat when he pulled in next to a magnolia outside a low apartment block and announced they'd arrived.

———

He hung his jacket over one of two chairs at the square table in the kitchen. The lounge room carpet was thin, stained, a mustard colour. She pushed the heavy drapes aside and looked out over the street and his car parked below to see the Space Needle framed by buildings.

She let the drapes drop. They smelled new, the only new thing in the apartment. 'You got any beer?'

He shook his head and folded himself into a corner of the orange sofa that looked like it was saved from the sidewalk. It faced a stereo, a pile of records on either side. His fingers, nails cut short, drummed on the armrest to an unheard beat.

The fridge was empty. The cupboard too.

'You don't do groceries?'

'I only just moved in. Plus, I eat out a lot.' He smiled and she shivered, took off her jacket and hung it over the other chair. Knelt in front of the LPs. Old stuff. Mostly live. BB King. Motörhead. Deep Purple. Hendrix. But there was some more recent stuff mixed in, TAD's newest among them.

'Thanks for helping me with the douchebag.'

'Happy to.'

Neither said he'd done nothing but watch and then drive, probably not even far enough to get the oil warm.

'You're a TAD fan, then?'

'Just trying to keep in touch.'

'In touch?'

He shrugged.

'Really.' She waved a Starship album at him.

'Not the same without Grace,' he said.

She slipped it to the back of the pile. 'What are you trying to get in touch with?'

He gestured towards the window. 'You know.'

His eyes were piercing. Her heart rate was going faster than the drums on *Touch Me I'm Sick*.

She opened a drawer, looking for a knife, a rolling pin, anything. Bare, all of them.

'It's not that late. We could go out …'

'Or we could stay in.'

He was standing, right there, in front of her, she hadn't heard him move, and the skin of her naked arms pimpled and the breath caught in her chest and her heart deafened her.

He reached out slowly, two fingertips gently alighting high on her left breast.

'You have blood on you.'

'Damn, that's hard to get out.'

He shook his head. 'I can do it.'

Her voice sounded reedy as she said, 'Can't fight, can't cook, but you can wash, hey.'

'Among other things.'

He leaned in, breath sour in that moment that his lips slipped past to caress her neck, and his hand flattened on her breast. The bite, when it came, was exquisite.

———

He gave her one of his t-shirts, a Dark Side of the Moon she could've put her finger through, and drove her home. Rest, he told her. Eat a steak.

Her father tore her a new one, her mother looked disappointed. She retreated gratefully to her room, earphones in, tape turned up, waiting for the exhaustion to claim her. But the ache in her arm wouldn't let her. She pushed up the sleeve of her jacket, marvelled at the cuts there, the smear of blood and saliva. He'd wiped it, tied a handkerchief around it, told her to keep her arm up, squishing the wound closed. A lucky escape, her gut told her. Very lucky indeed. She opened her fly and slipped her fingers down. She'd come like a storm when he'd opened her; now she was just wringing herself out, a gentle reprise, an image of his pale hairless chest, his dark hair as he bent over her, and the pain spiking into pleasures as teeth and tongue did their thing.

The proof was there in her arm, but was it true?

In the morning, she could see only the barest of marks where he'd bitten her. She wanted to ring Ruby, wanted to see her and gush it all out, but ... no, not even Ruby. Not until she was sure.

That night, she went back to the club and hung in the shadows, waiting for a likely mark. But he saved her the effort, the Chevy rumbling to a halt up the road. She made it to the door of the Off Ramp as he did. The bouncer held out a hand.

'She's fine,' Mr Contemplative said.

The bouncer said, 'Sure', and in they went. A nod to the door bitch and two stamps were provided for their wrists.

'Are you a Jedi?' she asked, and he said, 'What?', and leaned in closer so she could repeat it, but she didn't, her senses suddenly full of him.

He was wearing the same shirt, same jacket. Same smell. But his breath was of earth, wet and kind of mouldy.

'Buy me a drink?' she asked.

He raised an eyebrow.

She gave what she hoped was a salacious grin. 'I'll buy you one back.'

He put bills on the bar.

Two beers appeared before them. She swapped her empty glass for his.

'This can't become a habit,' he said.

'No?'

'I ... I don't hang around for long.'

'Don't worry, baby. I don't either.'

# BEBE LE STRANGE

1990: SEATTLE

He awoke at dusk, coming up out of the drowse, a twilight of the mind, peopled by memories. Smiled as *Louder than Love* played low and she hummed along. How many days was it now? Weeks?

She was at the table, bent over text books, a high school blazer draped over the back of the chair and a bag of groceries on the kitchen bench next to a pizza box. The room smelled of coffee, garlic paste, Starbucks with marshmallow – as much her perfume as the light scent she sprayed on her wrists despite his asking her not to. But he rarely drank from there anyway. He watched her through slitted eyes, the light through the dusty window over the kitchen sink illuminating her fringe as she pursed her lips, a frown wrinkling her brow as she tapped a pen against her teeth.

'Hey,' he said, startling her.

'Hey,' she said, and dropped the pen and slipped out of her check shirt as she crossed the linoleum on her sock feet, all she was wearing other than knickers. A Pluto tattoo peeked over the rim of her left sock; he kissed the blue butterfly perched on her hip as he pulled her to him.

He tasted, smelt, tomato sauce and cheese and dough, and

fake strawberry – a thick shake, probably – before her open vein washed it away.

After, as they lay there, a smear of blood on her breast and a fresh plaster over the slit high in her thigh, she asked, 'You really don't fuck?'

He shook his head.

She made a gesture with her mouth, one he was already coming to recognise, as though she'd bitten into something and was trying to work out what it tasted like.

'I bought pizza and coffee, toothpaste.'

'I don't eat, either.'

'Not ever?'

'It's unpleasant. The change, it makes it hard … we change.'

'But you must drink. Other than … you know.'

'If pressed, but it all comes out, one way or another. I don't need the bother.'

'Well, that all sucks. You still need to brush your teeth or gargle or something.'

'I don't think tooth decay is something I need to worry about.'

'Not for you. For me.'

'Oh. Well, sure.' He sniffed his armpit.

'Yeah, that wouldn't hurt either.'

She got off the sofa, found her shirt and poured a mug of coffee. 'You really don't mind?'

'Nope.'

'Doesn't upset you?'

'Not any more.'

She sat at the table, shirt hanging open, and twirled the pen.

'What are you working on?'

'Geography.'

'I was never much good at school.'

'I'm okay. Might do college. Journalism maybe. A music reporter would be cool. Getting to talk to all the bands, hear their albums first, get backstage.'

'What do your parents think?'

'Accountancy, reception. They're all about security. Dad works at Boeing, Mom's a bookkeeper.'

He tried to imagine her with that hair and that colour of nail polish at the front desk of an office. Heard ghosts of his conversations with his own parents, admired her strength and sense of purpose, neither of which he'd had at her age. Maybe still didn't.

'Have you told them about me?'

'What's to tell?'

He laughed as he walked over to peer over her shoulder at the text book, his desire stirring as he took in the contours of her, blood and sex teasing his senses.

'Would you like to see some geography?'

'Huh?'

'The night is young. I know a place in the mountains. We can be back by dawn.'

'I told my folks I was studying with a friend.'

'You are.'

She grinned. 'I guess. I'll need to ring them.'

'There's a pay phone down the corner. You should put pants on.'

'You think?'

They walked to the phone. He took in deep breaths of the city while she dropped in the coins and lied to her mother. What was he doing? Roy had been clear. It never lasts. It can't. They pass so quickly. They're never enough.

He should walk away. Disappear. Leave her to her geography, her dream of journalism.

But when she hung up and turned, he was still there, basking in her presence.

'So,' she said. 'Geography by night.'

# ROY: ON LIFE AND LOVE

Roy said, You know how people talk about Mexicans or Asians or blacks, how white people say they aren't like them? Well, that's hogwash. Of course they are. All taste exactly the same. But we ain't. We really aren't like them at all. We're the apex predator, right? I've heard of some of our lot who have taken on donors, rather than walk the night. Stay in, all domestic like. But here's the rub: however much they say they love you, how much they want it, that it's enough, it never is, never can be. Like any drug, it wears off. We are too different. No sun, no food, no children. Think about that. What do people need? All of those things. What do we need? Just one thing. And anyone will do. If you ever speak to the old ones, the ones with serious mileage, they'll tell you straight up: it's a bitch, getting old. Watching them all die. Watching the stupidity of it all, the pointlessness. And we're no better, just living because it's better than the alternative. Too ornery to just give it up. It's cold in the shadows, Chuck, and that's a fact, but it's still better than the grave. So keep on moving, that's my advice.

To which Charlie wanted to know, where that left him. Why had Roy taken him under his wing. What *was* Charlie?

To which Roy answered, An experiment. An accident. A lucky sonofabitch, or a cursed one, take your pick. The night,

Chuck, that's where we belong. It's the one thing that drives us on. And it means we ain't like them. Don't make the mistake of thinking any different because it'll get you killed. Worse, it'll break your heart, which is the same thing, really, just takes a mite longer.

# MAGIC MAN



Corey and Ruby were drinking toasted marshmallow lattes in Starbucks. Finally seated and a few mouthfuls in, Corey could finally blurt out that she was moving in with Charlie as soon as she finished school.

'Holy crap,' Ruby said. And then: 'What about college?'

Corey shrugged.

They'd been going to room together, Ruby doing art, Corey … English probably, of some sort. It was the only subject she was good at. Their music teacher said if she could give marks for enthusiasm Corey would be an A student, but you really needed some ability if not talent to get above a C. Thus did dreams die, as she wrote in a B+ essay.

'We should've run away together when we could,' Ruby said.

'Your folks aren't that bad.'

'But you're better.'

'Aw. I live at your place anyway.'

The only thing that kept her sane. She spent most nights at Ruby's where they had sleepovers in the basement and screamed along to Siouxsie and Nirvana and cut holes in their jeans and sewed patches on their jackets and did all sorts of things to their hair with scissors, razors and dye. They'd kissed a total of once, carried away on Ruby's clove cigarettes, a little weed and Lambrusco, and decided it hadn't been unpleasant but had been a tad weird. They gave shoulders to cry on after they'd slept with the latest loser. They smoked weed and wrote fuck-off lyrics in notebooks and drank cheap spirits and wine and whatever they could find that wasn't the same beer their dads drank.

'I can still stay over,' Corey said. 'And you can come visit.'

'Party at Ree's!'

'I can't wait to get away from the captain.'

Corey's name for her father, a walking cliché, a wifebeater-wearing, second-generation Seattleite working on a Boeing construction line while fiercely supporting his own father's faves, the Yankees. Sculling beers after work and regretting, loudly and often, his win-one-lose-one daughters, to the refrain of 'why can't you be more like your sister – at least she can throw a goddamn ball'. Her mother offered wan smiles and cupcakes honed at church. It took years for her to stop buying sundresses for Corey's birthday and finally buckled to band shirts or vouchers from Tower. On her 16th birthday her dad told her to keep her legs crossed (too late for that) and to get that ring out of her nose, with a 'typical' when she said her mom had okayed it (if an 'oh Corey, what have you done now' was indeed an okay; cue shouting match in the kitchen).

'What will you and Charlie do?' Ruby asked.

'Hang out.'

'I meant for money.'

'Whatever.'

'What, you gonna flash your tits on Aurora?'

Corey punched Ruby's arm, drawing an exaggerated 'ow'.

'I'll work at Mickey D's if I have to. Wait tables. Till something comes up. Charlie works.'

'I guess he's not that much older than you.'

She almost choked on her latte.

'What?' Ruby said.

'Age doesn't matter when you're in love, right?'

# JUST THE WINE



The morning of All Soul's Day, and she met Ruby at a characterless diner around the corner from their respective homes that served cheap hotcakes. She wore her devastated makeup from the night before like a badge, or maybe a wound, having splashed water and gargled before heading out in fresh underwear under blacks overdue for the tub. Her head still hurt and her eyes were dry burning.

They'd rolled up to Victor Moreno's manor on the hill, well, towards the bottom of the hill, but it had two storeys and his parents were hidden away upstairs like boogeymen while the kids rocked on to a mix tape of Billboard's best soft rock and New Romantic of the decade. Their host had gone minimal zombie, white face and torn clothes. Ruby had gone sexy vampire. Corey had gone as herself, her best Siouxsie eye makeup and fishnets under a tartan mini skirt her concession to the theme.

'Where'd you get to then?' Corey asked, gingerly sipping coffee that tasted as though it has been strained through her Cramps t-shirt.

Ruby at least had managed a shower, but there were dark

smudges under her eyes that hinted at not much sleep. 'You know Anika, right?'

'Art?'

Ruby gave a sly smile. 'Anyway.'

Corey shook her head, mumbled, 'Unbelievable.'

'What?' Ruby put down her fork, a mouthful of hotcake sodden with syrup still skewered, her brow furrowed with concern. 'Did something happen?'

'I think I barfed on Vic's carpet.'

'Oh shit, Ree!'

'I think the punch was spiked.'

'Like, you couldn't smell it?'

She shrugged. 'What else was I gonna do? If I heard *Blame It on the Rain* once more, I would've — well, I did, but after.'

'So?'

'Embarrassing.'

'What did he do?'

'He was nice. Called me a cab, even gave me the fare.'

'But he didn't try anything?'

'He didn't stick the cash down my bra, if that's what you mean.'

'Ree?'

'God, no, nothing happened. Just woke me up and sent me home. Like I said … nice.'

'Um, are you giving him a Mickey Mouse badge because he didn't rape you while you were passed out on his sofa?'

'That's not what I'm saying. Just, for a jock, he's okay.' She sipped, smiled. 'He might've given me his number.'

'You know he's a senior, right?'

'Of course! It was your idea to go to the stupid party. No doubt because Ms Hot Arts was gonna be there.'

Ruby picked up her fork, slid the food into her mouth, smirked.

'So, you gonna see him again?'

'He's nice, Ruby. Since when do I do nice?'

# DESIRE WALKS ON

## 1990: SEATTLE

She kissed him and ran a hand up his thigh and he braced himself. There'd been a girl at the movies who'd unzipped him and stroked him till he'd messed all over her fingers, making her laugh as she wiped herself on his handkerchief. Jerking off in his room and hiding the evidence so his mother wouldn't threaten him with Hell and his father accuse him of being a faggot. And since Roy, nothing. Memories flowing from the feel of her fingers on his denim thigh, but nothing else other than disappointment.

'C'mon.' A finger on his lips. 'No teeth. Just fucking.'

'I ...'

'C'mon, Charlie, you can still fuck, can't you? I mean, you're still a hot-blooded man, right?'

'Sure. Of course.' But the assertion rang false to him. He really wasn't sure what he was.

Her hand worked him as she kissed him and their tongues danced. And eventually his cock responded.

'There you are.'

She pushed him back and straddled him. Her body was hot and wet, her heart thudding, chemicals rolling off her in waves, and he wanted to lick the sweat from her tits and tear out her throat. She came and sat, breathing gentling, and then levered herself off and he rolled her and sank himself into her, her flesh opening under his teeth and the hot, hot blood gushing. He almost couldn't stop himself. He felt bad afterwards and brought her coffee in bed, then got takeout from the Chinese around the corner. He had to wash the sheets, but he could still see the stains even though she said she couldn't and he ended up throwing them out.

'You didn't come?' she asked afterwards, when the sweet 'n' sour was done.

'It was good. Very good.'

'But you didn't come.'

'That doesn't matter.'

'It matters to me.'

'As long as you enjoyed it.'

'I enjoy making you come – you know what I mean.'

'And you did.'

'Don't you miss it?'

'Not really, no. It's not that different.'

'It feels different.'

And later, much later, when he couldn't get it up no matter what she tried, she said, it's like fucking a meat dildo for all it does, and it wasn't long after that that they pretty much gave up on the sex thing and just concentrated on the feeding. He'd still stimulate her; the pheromones were a heady mix and he loved the way she tasted when her heart was running hot, but she left his cock alone and he was fine with that, it was one less thing to worry about.

# ROY: ON SEX

Some of us are quite the Lotharios, Roy said. Seduction is a great way to get what you need, and it can cover a multitude of sins. He grinned. Others are sadists. Others again are thugs, feeding off the fear and pain. They don't last long. Sometimes I think we're creatures of willpower, Chuck. Let's face it, what else do we have going for us, right? You have to be determined if you're gonna last.

Charlie wanted to know what he meant when he said they didn't last long.

To which he said, We're like any ecosystem, Chuck. We have our checks and balances. Keep your head down and don't make a mess and you won't have to worry about a thing.

A lesson, as it turned out, of the 'do as I say, not as I do' variety.

# THE NIGHT

## 1991: SEATTLE

They were on a blanket, the sky above full of stars, the city lights a corona to the west dimming the show. The fir trees whispered in a Pacific breeze that raised goosebumps on her arms and she snuggled closer into his side, but his body was cool under his parker. Their little fire sputtered and crackled, making his eyes shine redly but doing little to warm her.

'We should stoke the fire,' she said.

His body stiffened. 'You hear that?'

'What?'

'Sounds like … crying? Gasping?'

'Oh, it's probably lover's leap. That car park around the corner there? I got fingered for the first time there.'

'Maybe.'

'No, I definitely did. *Alone* was playing on his radio, which was kind of funny.' She snorted. 'He came in his pants and drove me home, worried about how he was going to sneak into the house and get his jocks and jeans clean without his mom noticing.'

He stood up, almost knocking her over.

'Hey.' She wrapped her arms around herself. 'What is it?'

'It's not right. Stay here, baby, I'll be right back.' He walked off towards the car park and she had to take two steps to his one to keep up. Like a robot, he was, in a straight line, his head cocked like a retriever. She still couldn't hear anything above the whispering trees and a jet coming into Sea-Tac. The city sparkled like sunlight on water, blinding almost, but he ignored the view, closing in on a silver Honda.

The windows were fogged but the rear passenger glass was smudged with a dark mop of hair.

Charlie reached for the door as the girl's protests reached Corey's ears. 'No,' she was saying, 'no, I don't want to, Reggie. Stop it.'

Corey's heart froze. God. There wasn't a phone in miles to call the cops. What could they do?

Charlie yanked at the door handle. It was locked. Of course it was. He tried the driver's door. Locked too. Corey pounded on the trunk.

'Hey, stop it, asshole, stop it right now!'

Glass shattered.

Corey jerked back.

Charlie reefed open the far-side passenger's door, hauled out a dude with his pants around his knees. Hauled him out and threw him on the ground like a landed fish, the boy gasping as he writhed in the attempt to get his pants up. Charlie leaned in, the girl screaming 'No', and Charlie telling her it was all right, he was there to help.

'Watch out,' Corey shouted as the boy found his feet.

The dude lunged at Charlie, wrapped an arm around his throat and punched him in the back.

Charlie turned and swiped with a backhand that caught the boy across the face and threw him right back into the dirt. Charlie kicked him in the guts, a couple times, until the boy just lay there groaning. Charlie knelt over him. A dark splash covered the boy's lower face.

'No, Charlie,' Corey shouted. 'Don't!'

She ran to him, made herself reach out and put a hand on his shoulder as he leaned over the boy, Charlie's body rigid and quivering. She could all but taste his hunger. Like a wolf, she thought, a wolf coming in for the kill at the end of the hunt.

The girl asked, her voice sobbing, 'What's going on?'

'Come on, Charlie,' Corey said. 'We need to get her home. Leave him. He's not worth it.'

Slowly, Charlie stood. He turned, then leaned down again, picked up a flick knife and threw it over the edge of the cliff to bounce into the dark. He shook his head.

'Okay,' he said. 'Okay.'

They drove the girl home. They offered to call the cops but she said she didn't want any trouble. Could do without *we told you so* from her parents and the hassle she'd get at school.

'Thanks,' the girl said, leaning in through the car window, and Charlie stayed in the car as Corey walked the girl to her door. When Corey got back in, she noticed.

'Holy shit, Charlie, you've got a hard on.'

He looked at his lap, as though noticing for the first time.

'Isn't it painful?'

He shrugged. 'It happens sometimes, when we're young, so I'm told. The excitement. Some kind of reflex.'

'Fucking take me home right now. Do not let that go.'

She threw him on the bed and stripped his jeans off, his cock still at half mast. She worked it, the flesh unusually warm for Charlie, and reckoned it'd do the job. She slipped on and rode him, the penetration acute, making her gasp, but it took a while, a long while, and she was sweating by the time she finally came. He wasn't even breathing heavy, just lying there, smiling, and he rolled her onto her back and buried his teeth in her, and he shuddered, but when she probed with a hesitant hand, she found only her drying juice on him, and his cock limp.

In the morning, she found his t-shirt, with four small tears in the lower back, each crusted with a lip of what made her think of black glue, but when she rubbed one it left an ochre smear on her fingertip. She shook him till he groaned.

'Charlie, did you get stabbed last night? Did that fucker *stab* you?'

He waved her away.

She rolled him over, so much dead weight, like a goddamn statue, but she got him there, to find his back unblemished, not even a dimple.

She poked her fingers through the holes, feeling the dry crusts scrape against her flesh, and shivered, all the way to her toes.

That night she said to him, 'Charlie, you could be a boxer. World champion. You could be anything.'

'No, I can't. Nothing that will make me stand out.' His gaze flicked to the records, then to the curtained window. 'I'm safe in mediocrity, under the radar.'

'You'll never be mediocre to me, Charlie.'

He drank from her again, then took her out for a burger, and she didn't even mind when the waitress cleaned up with a pointed, 'Not hungry, hon?', and he said with a smile, 'I ate already.'

# ROY: ON BLOOD



When it came to being a tour guide, Roy was pretty shit. Occasional mentions of people he'd met, businesses that weren't there any more, narrow escapes and great scores, but no sightseeing. So it was when they rolled into Seattle, any thought Charlie may have had of taking in the Space Needle under the comfort of the city's famously overcast skies quickly dashed. Another city, another dive, tonight's outing a mouldering hotel off Union Square, a haven still for skid row's lost and near penniless. Most cities had such a place, in Seattle referred to as the Underground after the precinct created when the streets were jacked up after the Great Fire. They were also shelters for what Roy called 'drifters', like them. A place to unwind, be themselves, and stock up on the finest forged identity documents an immortal could ask for. The price could come in cash or favours, and stays were kept short and infrequent.

They sat on a velvet lounge in the basement, wrapped in the scent of dust and candle wax, perfume, sweat, and blood. A couple played cards at a table nearby; Madonna's *Like a Virgin* played low on unseen speakers; a woman with scarred arms and a shock of green hair escorted another in a skirt suit and ruffled cuffs through a doorway.

'Why are we here?' Charlie asked, uncomfortable under the scrutiny of the others in the room, the music he didn't much care for, the feeling he was out of his depth, the two of them more like Brando (*Wild One*, not *Godfather*) than this MTV-tinged callback to olden times. Candles? Really?

Roy didn't answer, just took another sip of his aperitif of freshly drawn blood. Whet the appetite, he'd said. Hardly necessary, Charlie had thought, the real deal sitting only feet away at the bar, a young couple in leather pants and vests and way too much eye makeup.

Charlie put down his dainty glass, the gunk sticking to the sides. 'Why do they do it?'

'They like it,' Roy said, disparagingly. 'They like us, dream of being like us. And frankly, with that disease running rampant, we need places like this where we know the juice is pure.'

'So we *can* catch it.'

They'd done plenty of pick-ups as they'd worked their way up the coast, cashing up with bar work or security or, very occasionally, a minor robbery or burglary when Roy's uncanny ability to sway people to be generous let them down. A couple of months here, a couple more there, peppered with one-night stands and hitchhikers and short-term affairs, moving on just as Charlie was starting to feel settled in some kind of routine, Roy wary of letting the grass grow under his feet.

Charlie still preferred to slake his thirst with women, but Roy scoffed at his 'fussiness'. Blood was blood; the bottle it came in didn't matter. Unless, it turned out, the batch was off.

'The jury's out on that,' he said, gaze fixed on the vessels at the bar, 'and you can usually smell if something's off, just a taste, right, like I taught you. But there's the risk of us being carriers. No, Chuck, these days, we need them and they, in their own sad way, need us.'

The night before, at a nearby bookshop on an equally dilapidated block, Roy had handed over a suitcase of unknown contents in return for documents and a night or two of indulgence while they waited for delivery.

'We'll be heading east once the papers arrive,' Roy said. 'You ever been east?'

'Not even Utah.'

'Well, nothing missed there. Got a lot to show you, pal. Come on, let's get a decent drink.'

# HIJINX



Corey and Ruby were at a friend's place, and even though the music was turned up, some funk outfit Corey didn't know, they could hear their host moaning in his exaggerated gay-boy whine about how anybody on the monorail would be able to look straight into his lounge room once it was finished, and like he wanted to be looking out his window at cars full of tourists in Space Needle sweaters. The flat was foggy with smoke from cigarettes and spliffs, the kitchen bench a jumble of takeaway coffee cups, noodle boxes and booze.

The girls had staked out a sofa, interrupted occasionally by their host diving on Ruby to say how much he *loved* her work, how *far* she'd go, how he couldn't wait for opening night so she could *shine* with the others.

'Chuck working?' Ruby asked, a glass of cheap red in her hand, her nails freshly coated in shiny black.

'The Croc,' she said. 'He'll be along. What about Helena?'

'On shift. As usual.' She blew at her fringe, midnight black broken by a splash of crimson. 'Chuck should be here; this is a big night, Ree.'

'He'll be along,' she said again, and filled her glass, careful to keep the chipped side of the rim turned away.

'Just the two amigos then.'

'He'll be at the opening for sure. I put it on the fridge. So, here's to your exhibition, then.'

'My *shared* exhibition.'

'But you'll still *shine*.'

They laughed and clinked glasses.

'And here's to your story,' Ruby said with an exuberant toss of the glass that threatened to spill.

They clinked again, emptied their glasses, refilled.

'May there be many more for both of us.'

Ruby poked a finger at one of the magazines littering the coffee table amid ashtrays and bowls of dips and corn chips. 'Hey, you should apply for this, now that you're a published reporter.'

'God, Roo, it's just a zine. I could never write for *The Rocket.*'

'They can only say no. I mean, they put Ann Powers on and she was younger than we are. Just do it. Knock on the door and see what they say.'

The room filled. Two of Ruby's artist friends rolled in, dripping from rain, followed by a band who'd been getting some noise, all of them greeted by shouts of glee and raised arms and spilled drinks from their host. Soundgarden was singing *Show Me* when the gear appeared with a sly nod and crooked finger.

'You wanna?' Ruby said.

'I dunno.'

'Just come check it out.'

They wandered into the bedroom, Ruby leading with a gentle pressure on her forearm, where the spoon and syringe were being passed around.

A couple were already out, up against the wall, leaning on each other, and the host was slurring about making sure the needle was clean, *Jesus*, do you know *nothing*?

Corey pulled back. 'Charlie's always on about the drugs, y'know.'

'He's so square, Ree. Fuck, he's not even here. Let's just have a taste.'

But he was there, flying in with rain sparkling in his dark hair, like a raven in his trench and tee, a hand closing on hers.

'What the fuck do you think you're doing?' His jaw so tight, his eyes intense, his grip painful.

'We weren't going to—'

'Let's go, right now.'

Ruby tried to pull his hand off Corey's. 'She can make up her own mind.'

'Not if she takes that junk, she can't.'

He pulled Corey out, and Ruby stormed after them until her artist friends appeared like a swarm of spiders by her side, their cobweb sleeves draping around her, holding her back.

He and Corey huddled in the doorway of a closed Starbucks as the rain made patterns in the puddles of streetlight on the road.

'You don't control me,' she said. 'Treating me like that, in front of everyone.'

'Do you know what that shit can do to you? What it can do to me?'

'It's not that bad,' she said. 'We weren't gonna OD or anything!'

'Tell that to Stefanie.'

'You know damn well she choked to death.'

'Andy Wood, then?'

'That's just one.'

'Just don't, Corey. I mean it. I can't be with you if you're on it. It's just not safe for anyone.'

'If it means that much, okay, fine. Can we just go home now?' She wrapped her arms around herself, her coat still draped over the sofa at the party. 'I'm freezing my tits off.'

He gave her his coat and they started walking, hugging awnings where they could, the bare trees offering no cover.

'It's not as though I'm a junkie,' she said, after a bit, water dribbling down her neck and back.

'Sure you are,' he said. 'We both are. But trust me, heroin is worse.'

The shiver in his voice cut right through her like the wind coming off the sound, and she promised him, never, and back in the apartment, they showered and went to bed and kept each other warm.

# HOW DEEP IT GOES



The alarm went off and it was still dark out, drizzle trying to work its way up to actual rain. Corey flopped a hand out from under the covers to turn off the noise. Her uniform hung like a ghost from the rack against the wall, Charlie's discarded clothes a black shadow underneath.

She groaned, rolled to find him not in bed, light leaking from under the closed door. Her chest ached where he'd nipped her when he'd got home, could have been only a couple hours before.

So romantic, falling on her with the smell of tobacco and booze clinging to him.

God, she hated working the breakfast shift. She'd been out late, talking to a band for the magazine that got her the occasional review or interview. They'd smoked a little pot after, okay, during, and she'd almost got felt up by the oh-so-pretty bass player, such long fingers working her fishnetted thigh like a fret board. Roo's fault; she'd been meant to drop by and collect her, but had blown her off for a night in with her squeeze, Helena, who was almost finished her medical degree, so – no more jokes about the age gap, Ms Freshman.

Corey stumbled out to the living room. Charlie was reading

a *Rolling Stone* by lamplight, in shorts and boxers, impervious to the cold leaking in through the closed window.

She waved, he smiled, she showered, dressed, drank the coffee he'd made for her, found him crept into bed when she went to unplug her phone from the bedside charger. She curled against him for a moment, wishing she could feel his breathing, but he was as still as a statue though the sun hadn't come up, not that she could tell past the curtains and the newspapers they'd taped to the windows.

He'd groan in his sleep sometimes, especially during the day, mostly during the day, when the soft sunlight managed to penetrate their defences. Kicked in his sleep, even shouted.

She kissed his shoulder and fumbled into her raincoat and let herself out. Standing hunched against the rain at the bus stop, traffic sluicing past, it all felt unreal, like he was a figment of her imagination, a romantic delusion. Until the sun went down and there he would be, his smile making her heart beat faster.

# ROY: LETTING ME DOWN AGAIN

## 1988: SURPRISE, AZ

Charlie came home, ears and chest still delightfully aching from the bass assault, and his nose told him something wasn't right. The stench of blood was rolling down the stairs like a ghostly waterfall, and the high of the gig flipped to anxiety, his ears now pounding, his hearing deafened. He ran to the door and fumbled it open, keys jingling like a jailer's. Roy was sprawled on the floor in front of the sofa, red and sticky with blood, and slumped on the sofa was a young man with a piece of hose tied high on his arm, leaking from his throat and arms and chest, a chocolate fountain gone hideously wrong.

It took only a moment, stepping carefully as though the drying stains on the rug were land mines, to confirm the boy was dead, the plate and needle and spoon still by his side. Charlie's vision was awash with red. He forced himself to drag Roy up out of the mess, the blood smearing his fists where they grabbed the man's sodden button-up shirt, open to the waist.

'What the fuck have you done, Roy?'

Roy lolled in his grip, staring towards the ceiling, drooling pink from a shit-eating grin.

It took ages to clean it up, a nerve-wracking early-morning drive into the desert with a shovel. Promises of never again.

Until the next time.

And the time after that.

'Why don't you try it for yourself?' Roy said. 'It makes it all go away.'

'How is this going away? I thought we had to live quietly, under the radar.'

'No one's going to miss junkies.'

'Someone's got to notice eventually. Even hobos got friends. And then what?'

'You've got no idea, you little punk! Our life means being on all the time, hearing and smelling and tasting everything that we can't have. In terms you might understand, it's turned up to eleven. This switches it off. And sometimes I lose control, fine. So what? They breed like fleas. More for us.'

'I need to leave.'

'You can't survive by yourself and you know it. One word from me, the Underground will shun you. You'll wither and wither until there's nothing left for you but a sun bath. So don't preach at me, don't presume to tell me how to live. You're not so pure.'

'Jesus, I did weed. Everyone does weed.'

'No different, Chuck. An escape, just not as effective. Seriously, I've never felt anything like it. So don't knock it till you've tried it. And don't forget, you need me.'

Roy sat in the car while Charlie dug the holes.

# THESE DREAMS



Clinton was on the television, bravo, whatever. Charlie had seen the posters, him and Dole on power poles and hoardings. Could imagine his father ranting; all the more reason not to care. He stumbled out, shrugging off the stupor of day, a rare night off for the two of them together, a club, a stroll by the water maybe. But Corey wasn't in the lounge room, light and smell drawing him to the bathroom instead.

In an old check shirt in front of the mirror, hands in plastic gloves smeared with green, hair still clumped in the sink. She bounced the sodden emerald locks. The smell of fresh dye wafted around her.

'You've changed your hair.'

'Like it?'

'Green with envy,' he said, eliciting an eye roll.

Maybe she picked up on something deeper than the pun, because she asked, 'What do you mean?'

'I can't do that.' He stroked a wet strand of hair, then traced the latest tattoo on her arm, a smiley face turned ill with crosses for eyes and its tongue sticking out of a wobbly smile. 'Or this.'

He pushed her hair aside to reveal her neck. His hands found her breasts as his teeth opened her vein. She sagged against him and the wetness of her hair was cold against his chest, a runnel of green dye mixing with the trickle of blood that escaped him.

He remembered, early on, Roy telling him, nothing changes, and how he'd sliced at his arm, bloodless and almost painless, the flesh slowly knitting to an unmarked surface. Slashed his hair back to a bleeding scalp, only to have it return as it had been in the morning, as though the dawn came with.

Suddenly he realised she was no longer a teenage girl; she was a woman, her body filled out, her attitude more serious, her vision starting to lift to the future. She hadn't voted, but only because she thought they were both dicks.

———

At least Charlie was cheap to keep, but grocery shopping for one could be kind of a drag. He would watch her eat and drink, piss sometimes, sleep, reminding her of a dog or a cat, ear cocked, frowning, as though wondering what sorcery this was. Hopeful of a morsel from the table, aware it was not good for them, lustful just the same.

All he needed was fuel for the car – the car in which they drove at night to wherever the whim took them (as long as they were back by dawn, though he could curl up in the trunk if needed), the seats musty, radio tuned to the End – and more recently his beat-up bike, to her mind kind of skeletal and somehow ironic, the red Triumph badge on the tank defiant for someone who couldn't stand the sun.

They made do, with what he brought in, what she made at the diner and the occasional review, though the latter was usually paid for with her name on the door and a free drink. She was thinking maybe she should've gone to college with Ruby, wondering what doors it might've opened, how Charlie would've fit into that scene, when there was a jangle from the front and a pause and a male voice saying, 'Holy cow, is that Corey? Corey Vee?'

She looked up from the table she was wiping, aware it was

still an hour till close, and Victor Moreno was standing there with two pals in jeans and pullovers, hair still short like it was in high school, his clothes tight, all-American.

'Fancy seeing you here,' he said as the two dudes pulled up in a booth and flipped the menus.

The burn in her cheeks took her by surprise. Apart from Ruby and a couple of her hangers on, she didn't associate with anyone from school, never had really, and suddenly she was acutely aware that she had been waiting tables since working the drive-through in her freshman year. Character building, her dad said, to earn her own money, get out of the house, meet people.

'Hi,' she said.

He introduced himself. 'From school. You were into art, right?'

'That was Ruby. I was the writer.'

'Was?'

'I do a bit still.'

He nodded.

'Still got the coloured hair.'

'Still got it.'

He smelt of cologne, beer.

'What are you after?'

He grinned, avoiding being salacious, but still, something there in his eyes, that turn of the lips. 'What do you recommend?'

'Burgers are all right.'

'I'll have a burger then.'

She told him to take a seat and he shoved in next to one of his pals and she wrote their orders and hustled back to the kitchen. For some reason she didn't understand, she comped him a soda and stumbled through small talk in between serving the few other customers, drew a blank on enquiries about schoolmates and feigned interest in the ones he was still in touch with, found out he wasn't married, and that he was a cop, which figured, him being so straight, but not straight enough not to serve booze to a ninth grader at a Halloween party.

He hung around until his friends dragged him out,

bouncing club names around as to where to next, and he left a good tip and his phone number on a napkin, his cologne lingering as she wiped the table clean. For a moment there she'd thought he might've been about to ask her to join them, still keen to be seen out with the freak, but maybe she'd imagined it, his wingmen guiding him to a safe exit. Would she have gone? They'd laughed a lot, the three of them, still boyish, jostling, joking. Charlie didn't laugh much, not even at the TV, as though the jokes passed him by. Still, he did other things with his mouth that no one could.

She eyed the napkin, thoughts swirling around school and the college that wasn't, unable to remember if the number was different to the one he gave her after she barfed in his house. There was a zero in the number, and she cupped the napkin hard, drawing two eyes and a crooked nose and two fangs on it, pressing so hard she tore it. She locked up, dumped the trash outside, napkin included, and headed for home. But Victor had got her thinking, this blast from the past that never was, got her thinking about the future. She and Charlie were both stuck, him in the night, she with a foot in two worlds but belonging to neither. Her stomach growled at the hot sauce she'd sprinkled on the last fries of her shift, highlighting the big difference between her and Charlie: her clock was ticking.

# HIGH TIME



They were playing *Nevermind* and Corey's sister had a candle lit in front of the album sleeve, propped up near the stereo. Even though Maya would never dream of letting her knees show through ripped jeans, let alone wear plaid, music was a tie that bound them.

'Four years,' Maya said, shaking her head, Courtney on her hip, the baby's chin shining with drool.

Corey glanced at Charlie, over by the barbecue with her dad and Maya's husband, Dave. 'Live fast, die young …'

'I'm his age now.' Maya shook her head again and the baby gurgled at the motion. 'I can't imagine leaving little Courtney.'

'You can never know what's going on, you know, in someone's head.'

'Something you wanna tell me, sis?'

'God, she's so goddamn cute.'

'Feeling clucky?' That teasing grin, so familiar, pre-dating braces and boyfriends.

'Hell no.'

'How are you two going?'

'We're good.'

'Does he ever change his hair? Like, ever?'

'Charlie's very comfortable in his own skin.'

'I like yours.' She ran her fingers through Corey's coloured locks, her hand smelling of baby powder and menthol cigarettes. 'I just can't be bothered.'

Courtney snagged her mother's short hair, leaving a strand of drool between split ends and her stubby little fingers.

Maya rolled her eyes. 'You want another drink?'

Mother hovered by the cooler as they collected dripping cans from the ice water. 'Here,' she said, hands out for her granddaughter. 'You and Charlie,' Mother said over the baby's shoulder. 'How long's it been now?'

'Since?'

'Since you were together? Is it eight years?'

'Nine, mother.'

She tsked, still smiling at the cherub in her grip. 'I'd like another grandchild. One for each hand.'

'You heard the woman,' Maya said. 'Get to it.'

Corey groaned, said, 'Let me check my diary; I think I'm free next Tuesday.'

'Corey!' Then Mother frowned. 'He should marry you. It has been long enough. More than long enough.'

'It won't matter, will it? The millennium and all that?'

'Don't be silly,' Maya said. 'Nothing's gonna happen.'

Courtney started to cry and she reached to take her back. 'Will it, bubba? It's exciting being here for it. I mean, it's not like we'll be here for the next one, will we? Although I guess Courtney might, the way medicine is going. Even Granma might, she'll outlive all of us!'

'God will not allow a computer to end his world, Corey,' Mother said.

'Not the world, Mom. Just us.' She glanced at Charlie, staring distractedly at the barbecue flames. 'Mostly.'

'You should marry, have children,' Mother steamrolled on. 'Your sister can't do it all.'

'Of course she can. She's Maya.'

'Don't,' Maya said.

Father shouted from the barbecue, 'The wieners are ready', and they all gathered round the table.

'You need to eat,' Mother told Charlie. 'You're too thin.' She pinched his arm.

'I have a delicate stomach, Mrs Vee.'

'Eat yoghurt. Marry my daughter. Have babies.'

'In that order?'

Dave, a tear of mustard in his beard, said, 'All in good time, hey. It took me three years to reel Maya in.'

'Like a fish?' she snapped.

'Just like that.' He raised a can in her direction. 'I reckon it was my coffee making that won the day. All those foam hearts.'

She held the child out. 'She needs changing.'

Mother tsked, but he put the can down and took the kid inside.

Maya lit a cigarette.

Charlie wrinkled his nose.

'You want one?' She offered the pack.

'Not near my food,' Mother said, waving her away.

'Seriously, Charlie, I can't believe she's still with you,' Maya said. 'We all thought Corey would be, you know, different. Gay maybe.'

Mother's hands flew to her chest as though her heart was about to bust loose. 'Maya!'

'One of those lesbos,' she said, blowing smoke. 'Like Ruby. How is Ruby? Still moving to New Orleans with her lady doctor?'

'She sure isn't,' Charlie said.

'What, moving?' Maya said.

'Gay. Corey. She isn't.'

'You're so quaint, Charlie,' Maya said. 'I never figured CeeCee to fall for such a quaint guy.'

Corey took his hand. 'Charlie isn't quaint.'

'No,' Mother said, 'he'd have married you by now.'

'Now, Mother,' Father said in his deep rumble. 'Corey has her career to think about, and women can have babies much later nowadays. Not like in our day.'

Charlie checked his watch. 'Hey, I'm real sorry, but my shift is starting in like a half hour.'

'Always rushing off,' Mother said.

'You want a beer or a dog for the road, Charlie?'

'I'm good, thanks Mr Vasilakis.'

'God,' Maya said. 'I wish I had his skin. Serious, CeeCee, it's like he hasn't aged a day since the two of you hooked up.'

'Good genes, I guess.'

'You'd have a beautiful baby, the two of you.'

'It's really not on the radar, sis.'

'Worried about the millennium bug? Seriously?'

'It's just … no.'

'Clock's ticking, CeeCee. It's the best thing, really it is. You can still write your stories with baby puke on your blouse.'

Dave came back, the kid asleep against his chest.

'Charlie has to go,' Mother said.

Dave nodded. 'Do you think we should take this one home? Enjoy the silence while it lasts.'

'The best thing, really?' Corey said.

'Don't let the black rings around my eyes fool you,' Dave said. 'I love this little monster more than you can imagine. You should have one of your own so they can grow up together. Best cousins.'

'Wouldn't that be something?' Corey's mother pressed a tea towel of food into her arms. 'Eat something, Corey. You're too thin. The two of you. You need to keep your strength up.'

Charlie jangled the car keys. 'Baby?'

'Coming.'

'God, don't you get sick of the night shift?' Maya asked.

'We did our share,' Dave said.

'And I don't miss them one bit. CeeCee?'

'It's a drag, sure, but you know, Charlie's been doing it for so long now, I don't think he could live any other way.'

# ROY: THE FINAL DEATH

1988: SURPRISE, AZ

It was only a week later, or so he supposed, thinking back, comparing concert tickets stuck in a battered album; he was in their shoddy dive trying to get his head around *Music for the Masses*, the needle finding *Never Let Me Down Again* over and over, the power pirated from the corner post, when Roy charged in. The day was a threat through the curtains, grey light blasting through the door, making his vision dance with stars as the door slammed them back into the murk.

'Get your things, pronto. We gotta make tracks.'

'What the fuck?'

Roy picked him up one-handed, the t-shirt tearing in his grip.

'Get your shit together.'

Spittle flecked Charlie's face. Roy's eyes were red-rimmed and bloodshot, the whites pink, the lips full, cheeks blushed crimson and road-mapped with lines.

'Fuck, Roy, what've you done?'

'Just get in the goddamn car.'

'It's daylight. We can't—'

Roy hit him, sending him sprawling, and he heard the crack of an LP where he landed hard.

'I'm leaving in two minutes and you don't want to be here after I'm gone.' Roy grabbed a revolver from the bedside drawer, checked the cylinder, slapped it closed. 'Trust me, Chuck. Get your shit together. Two minutes.'

It didn't take two minutes. They were always ready to move on, and they didn't have much to pack. The record player and the LPs he could gather into their boxes came first, his fanny pack of cash and IDs, the backpack of clothes, his shot glass and half bottle of bourbon for those times he liked to pretend.

He stood at the door laden like a trail mule, digging in his heels. 'It's daytime.'

'Stop your whining! Just run to the car and get in the back.'

Roy was covered head to toe, the balaclava and ski mask looking ridiculous, this far from the mountains, in summer. The revolver was in his waistband, a box of documents peeking from the top of a hastily filled rucksack looped across one shoulder.

'How far do you think we can get like this?' Charlie asked.

'Far enough. Now get if you're getting.'

Charlie got. Gear in the boot, then covering himself in a blanket on the back seat as the car rocked to Roy's weight in the driver's seat, the car roaring off, fish tailing at the corner.

The heat pushed Charlie down as Roy drove in silence, just the rumble of tyres on road, a faint whistle from air over a hole, the smell of hot road and oil almost soporific in the dusty twilight under the blanket.

Another car growled up beside them, matched them.

'Fuck,' Roy said. The thump of fists on wheel. 'Fuck, fuck.'

The thudding of wheels slipping off tarmac onto gravel verge, a stone dinging on the underside like a rifle shot, and Charlie struggling to emerge from his stupor as a beam of sunlight washed across the cloth over his head and he heard, felt, Roy being dragged from the car. That got him up, wrapped in the blanket like some Mexican at siesta, standing at the back door on legs turning molten in the heat.

Three men in leather and jeans, dragging Roy away from the road into the sun-washed rocks and sand.

'He was told,' one said, crossbow in his hands, falling back to watch Charlie. 'He had his chance. Don't make the same mistake.'

Charlie took a step, could see over the roof that Roy had something in his chest; they were dragging him by the arms, his head down, bouncing, his feet leaving twin tracks.

'Who are you?' Charlie asked, his voice hoarse from his dry throat.

'Concerned citizens. Now just get back in the car. Leave quiet when you can.'

Charlie crawled back in.

'Good boy.' The man threw the keys into the footwell and slammed the door. 'Take Arizona off your map. Or that'll be you.'

# CITY'S BURNING



MTV was on and she was sitting through Christina, waiting for Korn, when Charlie slumped down on the sofa beside her.

'I don't know how much longer we can stay in Seattle,' he said.

'The protests weren't that bad,' she said, snorting.

'You know it's got nothing to do with that.'

'Is this about my parents?'

'In a way. Your family, your friends … they're getting suspicious. People are looking at us when we hold hands.'

'So you're my toy boy.'

He raised his eyebrows.

'I don't want to leave Seattle,' she said. 'Everyone I know is here.'

'It's not just your people. It's mine, too.'

'Who are your people, Charlie?'

'Roy, he taught me the signs. Just graffiti, mostly, like dogs pissing on trees, marking our territory. It's all about being unobtrusive. We're sharks but we can't break the surface, see? No fuss, that's what we're about. And keep moving. I told you about this. Gotta keep moving.'

'What about me?'

'You come with me. It's kind of fun, getting to know a new place.'

'What about my job?'

'New York? That's where all the publishers are, right?'

'There's nothing happening on the East Coast. God, it's probably gonna be all Britney and boy bands anyway.'

'There's Latin. Hip hop.'

She poked her tongue at him, with accompanying eye roll.

'You can get another job. You're good!'

'But my sister's just had her baby. My niece ...'

'You can always come back and visit.'

'You think they don't want to see you too?'

'I think they can do without it. I'm too thin, I haven't married you ... and I can't have a grandchild for your mother to fawn over.'

'Shit, Charlie. You really expect me to pack up and start again?'

'I thought you'd like it. That you didn't want to be a housewife or a plain Jane. Your family drives you insane. That's what you said. Too controlling, not allowing you to be yourself.'

'That was almost ten years ago, Charlie. They've changed. I've changed.'

'But I haven't. I can't.'

'No. I guess this isn't what you expected either. I mean, what were you going to do – before?'

'Before Roy?'

She nodded.

'I was just a kid. I wanted to play music, do up cars, get high, get laid.'

'So what about the music? I've never even seen you with an instrument.'

'It's just not practical.'

'You could put it on the world wide web.'

'So Napster can rip me off?'

'I'm serious here.'

'Like that Lestat guy in the books? I don't have the hair.'

She hit him in the arm. He pretended it hurt.

'Still, we don't have to decide yet, do we? I really want to see in 2000 here. That's only a few months away.'

'I guess we can try to ride it out for a bit longer. But people are beginning to notice. Start thinking about where else you'd like to see. If you're coming.'

'I don't want to lose you.'

'Here's a map, if that helps.'

She unfolded the paper he took from his shirt pocket, frowned as she took in the scribbled notes in different colours and types of ink, even a heavy pencil. Dates, rings around towns and cities, cities mostly, West Coast.

'So I don't lose track. There's a lot of blank places still,' he said. 'I'm thinking Vancouver. A bit of a scene there, the weather's nice. And it's not too far away, if you wanted to come back and visit.'

'Vancouver.'

'Think about it. But you'll need to decide soon.' He flashed a smile, but it ended in a grimace. 'Because I'm not getting any older.'

# TUNING UP

He'd thought then he might make a guitarist, but didn't even have a guitar any more. Where was the point? He couldn't perform, not with an ageless face. He'd smashed one instrument when he'd realised the irony, of having all the time in the world to practise and no way to take it on the road. A real fly-by-night tour? Another guitar he sold for a new driver's licence. Sometimes he thought – schemed – that he could get a frontman or woman, someone to play his music to the masses while he worked the magic in the studio. Maybe studio only? The mysterious Charlie, reclusive musical genius. The Gibson had made a satisfying sound as it broke into pieces, but he'd cried after.

# WHAT ABOUT LOVE

## 2000, SPRING: SEATTLE

They were at her sister's to celebrate Courtney's second birthday, just the family. A pair of yellowthroats twittered in the hedge, as sure a sign of spring as the arrival of the swallows. Late afternoon sun rayed across the back lawn like a lighthouse beam. The family had stopped ribbing Charlie about his hoodie to move outside and fry hamburgers, a single dead balloon high in a tree and some rain-ruined streamers reminders of Courtney's early birthday party at the weekend that had filled the yard with a flock of toddlers.

Corey leaned against the porch rail, the peeling timber aglow in the sunlight, a beer in her hand as the aroma of charring meat wafted across the yard.

'She's grown quickly,' Charlie said from the old wicker lounge in the shadows near the door. Staying awake during the afternoon had been a struggle for him, passed off as 'jet lag' from working nights, but the family was used to his daytime lassitude. They only visited her parents on occasions, but she enjoyed playing aunty for little Courtney and doing the odd babysitting run. The kid had brought her and her sister closer, if Charlie had helped keep the divide between her and her parents too wide to properly bridge.

'I know,' she said. 'I can't believe it's 2000.'

'And the world didn't end.'

'Give it time. They cancelled New Year's at the Needle, after all.' She drank while she stared at her niece and her sister, dodging her mother's glare where she sat on a garden lounge with her father, who seemed as tired as Charlie under his straw hat.

'God. I'm almost thirty, Charlie. What've I got to show for it?'

He stepped over to squeeze her hand, then quickly withdrew from the patch of sunshine. 'We're having fun, aren't we?'

'If you count waiting tables and getting drunk at gigs, sure, but it's hardly a retirement plan.'

'You've got your writing.'

She turned, bare crop-top shoulders in the sun, feeling a chill evening breath already. 'The mags are dying like hip hop gangsters, and I just can't seem to get a break.' She sighed. 'I mean, it's fun, sure, but I need more.'

His gaze slid from hers, towards the bushes and those cheerful birds. Seeing … what? She could guess. Herself with grey hair and tits down to her knees and a walking frame, and Charlie, still twenty, still hungry.

He returned his gaze to her, as though reading her thoughts. 'Have you thought of going somewhere. To start over?'

She shook her head. 'I don't know what I want.' But she did know. She didn't want to die. The thought made her shiver.

'You want your pullover?' he asked.

She took a long swig, swallowed deliberately, trying to taste the Bud, but it was her third and any flavour had long faded to something akin to rotting leaves.

'You sure you can't give me what you've got?'

'We've talked about this.'

'You're sure, though. I mean, you came through it.'

'Roy said it's, like, one in a hundred. A thousand, maybe.'

Courtney shrieked and then chuckled as her father threw her in the air and caught her, and Corey's sister shouted, 'These patties are about done, you two. Get your butts over here.'

Corey waved, turned back to Charlie, drained the last of her beer.

'I think I want a baby.'

He stared for a long moment, his eyes almost red in the low sunlight. 'I'm not sure that's a good idea, Core.'

'Didn't you ever want to be a father?'

'It was only ever a thought. I was twenty when … My mom was as bad as yours, but I wasn't even going steady with anyone. Not much of a market where I grew up, and I thought I had time, for cars, for music, to see something before I settled down.'

'And you've never seen them since? Your parents?'

'Nope. '

'Not even a peek?'

He shook his head.

'Your mom?'

'Too hard. She wanted to be a grandma so bad. This … she wouldn't cope with this. The music was bad enough.'

'They must be so worried.'

He shrugged. 'My old man and I didn't get on. I mean, really didn't get on.'

'That's too bad. You think maybe you should?'

'Too much water under that bridge. Let the sleeping dogs lie. Imagine if I turned up now, just like I was when I left – they'd die of a stroke.'

She snorted, tasted beer in her nose, coughed. 'You would be a good dad, Charlie. We could be good parents. Better ones. You could stay up with the kid at night. Split shifts. It'd work.'

'How? I can't see us being allowed to adopt.'

She pushed off from the rail to cup his face. 'I've still got it, baby.'

His eyes tightened. His skin was cold as steel.

'Don't do this, Corey. Please.'

She stepped back and crossed her arms. 'I've given you everything, Charlie. Everything. You need to give me this.'

'It's just not safe. Look at what happened to Roy and me.'

'What happened, Charlie? You won't talk about it, just wave

it around like a big flag: don't do this, don't do that, you won't wanna end up like Roy. He's like some kind of boogeyman.'

'Just trust me. It's not safe. Really, it isn't.'

'Nothing's safe, Charlie. Going to school isn't safe, crossing the road isn't safe, flying isn't safe. But I want this. I'll risk it because it's worth it.'

'Even if we could raise a kid, there has to be another way. A better way.'

'You feed from other people. This is no different. Just…a little more to show for it.'

He jerked to his feet. 'You got someone in mind? Someone at the office? Some muso take your fancy?'

'Oh, please. I love you. But this is the one thing you can't give me that someone else can.'

'What? Sex? You said it wasn't that important.'

'It isn't. A means to an end, that's all. But it would give me someone to grow old with.'

'You're already—'

'You know what I mean, Charlie.'

He was quiet for a long time, slouched back against the wall in the shadow, arms crossed.

'Do you want to leave me? For a husband. A warm one.'

'No, of course not.' She took his arms. 'I want us to share this.'

'You said it yourself. We're waiting tables and pouring beers. How can we even afford a kid, let along raise one safely?'

'We'd manage. Just like everyone else.'

'But I'm not like everyone else.'

'This might get you a little bit closer. Did you ever think of that? Someone else to care for?'

'I care for you.'

'A kid's different.'

'You know we can't stay here, Core. How would you cope?'

'When it comes to that, I would. We would.'

He shook his head, staring off again, over her shoulder.

'I'd never have to see the…the donor again. Just another one-night stand. I can pick 'em.'

He grinned wryly. 'You didn't always.'

'I'm wiser than I was then.' She kissed him. 'It'd give you something to do for the next twenty years—'

'And when our kid looks older than me?'

'We'll work it out.'

He shook his head again, then caught her gaze, his stare intense. 'I didn't want to need you this bad.'

She held her breath, aware of him standing right on the edge.

'I don't want to lose you,' he said.

She breathed out, in, sensing him step back. 'You will eventually. Unless…this would be the next best thing, Charlie.'

He ran his hands through his hair, the tussle slowly settling back into its usual style. 'The risk—'

'The kid would be my legacy. Our child. Ours, Charlie.'

'I'm not sure I can even be a father.'

'Who is? You don't know until it happens, then you do the best you can.'

Her sister and niece were shouting at her. Her brother-in-law, waving a burger at them, said, 'What are you two talking about that's more important than these little bad boys?'

She took his hands. 'Believe me, no one's more surprised than me, but I want it, Charlie. I need it.'

'If this is what it takes, then okay.'

She kissed him, held him. 'It'll be all right, Charlie, you'll see. You'll be a great dad. Just think how good you'll be helping the kid with his, or her, history lessons!'

She dragged him into the soft sunlight, a neighbour's maple throwing a helpful shadow, and her sister asked what she was so happy about, but Corey didn't answer, just splashed on ketchup and mustard and dove in as though she was already eating for two.

Charlie took a burger but didn't eat it, but they were used to that.

# CHARLIE'S LETTER C.1974

Dear Mom and Dad,

Sorry if I have scared you with my absence. I know the phone call that other day must've worried you, with the breakdown and all, but I am safe up here. I have met someone and we are travelling and working our way around for a bit. Not a hippie, I swear! tell Dad not to pop a gasket. I will be in touch from time to time and pray you stay well and forgive me for being ~~so impet~~ a jerk.

Your son,
Charles jr

# ALL I WANNA DO IS MAKE LOVE
# TO YOU

## 2000, AUTUMN: SEATTLE

He was trudging by the side of the road, head down against the rain, no umbrella, not even a coat. Cropped hair slicked to his skull, the pale of his shoulders showing through his saturated shirt. She pulled up a little way ahead and reached over to wind down the window. Rain splattered in through the gap, the cold rush of air raising goose bumps. He looked set to walk past. She called out. Let the car idle forward to keep pace. Tried again.

'You need a lift?'

He looked sideways at her, water-slick face waxen in the grey glow of headlights and distant streetlights through the rain. She shivered. Strong stubbled jaw, staring eyes red-rimmed, lips pulled in a line. His chest seemed to fill the window behind his visage, and heat rushed through her.

Recognition struck like a match, and that was her moment, in the sudden flare, before he made the connection: to just accelerate away. Her foot stayed where it was, numb mind slowly churning.

'I'm just walking,' he said eventually, and a glimmer of a smile broke through his blue lips.

No turning back.

'You'll catch your death.'

He gave a laugh, reminding her of Charlie, some inside joke.

'That's very kind but …'

He straightened and stepped back, wet cloth on muscle above the belt and trousers.

She opened her door and stood to look at him over the roof. She shuddered in the shock of cold rain on scalp and nape, penetrating her collar.

His eyes narrowed, his mouth opened.

'C'mon, Victor. Let me buy you a coffee. Give you a chance to tell me why you're just walking out here in the rain.'

'Corey Vee? What are the fucking odds?' He pushed a hand through his dripping hair, shook his head, looked away, looked back. She thought she saw something shift, like Paul on the road to Damascus maybe, felt something reciprocate, tightening her lungs. What were the chances indeed?

'C'mon, what can it hurt?' she said, her voice coming from miles away. 'Now that we're both wet?'

He laughed again, lighter this time, and again ran a hand pointlessly through the hair clinging to his forehead like seaweed.

'Sure,' he said. 'Why not? Though where you'll find anywhere this time of night out here—'

'I know a place.'

---

What he lacked in finesse he made up for with energy and enthusiasm. Desperation, even. It surprised her, how much she'd missed the heat and the sweat, the connection, the friction. He wanted to talk, to catch up, but she shut that down with bare flesh and urgent lips. It was just for one night, she told him, and his agreement came as she stripped the sodden shirt from his body. They drank from the poor options in the minibar and let their bodies do the talking, whispers building to shouts, surge and subside, and it was all she could do to stay awake when he finally nuzzled into sleep beside her, her thighs and cunt gently aching. Two puckered scars on his chest she wanted to ask about as she had licked them, a secret she'd never know now, as she slipped out from under the covers, dressed hastily and minimally for the jog back to the car, pausing only by the little desk near the door to scribble on the pad, afraid the scratching of the pen would wake him. That air of vulnerability and strength, a suggestion of danger in the eyes and jaw, reminded her of Charlie: if he had grown past twenty, had worked out, had joined the Marines maybe. Oh. She stared through the streaked windscreen at the blurred neon of the hotel sign as she found the packet of Kool and lit one up with a shaky hand, then cracked the window open as though it might help the smell escape. She jerked her gaze to the mirrors when she heard a motorcycle, but she never saw it, and the growl quickly faded under the hammer of rain on the roof.

# (BEAT BY) JEALOUSY

2000, AUTUMN: SEATTLE

He wheeled the motorcycle into the carport and ran upstairs, the bike foolish perhaps for a night rider in a city prone to rain, but worth it for the freedom it gave him, especially when Corey needed the car when she was working late, or like tonight, prowling, and forbidding him from keeping watch over her despite the obvious risks. He understood she wouldn't want him as a witness, and perhaps it was more perversity on his part than a desire to protect her that drove him to shadow her on her trysts. Like cutting himself to see if he could bleed.

He'd only just beaten her home, city lights distorted through the water on his visor, his Trident chewing up the distance quicker than her car as she dawdled through the slick streets. He was getting a pot of coffee on when she came in, shaking rain from her coat, the water making beads in her hair under the fluoro light.

'You're home,' she said, seeming surprised.

'We closed early. The weather, I guess.' He leant against the kitchen bench, hoping he looked nonchalant as the lie slipped easily from his tongue. 'Coffee?'

'Sure.'

The reek of cigarette and beer wafted from her, and deep

under, the musk of recent sex, blood in her cheeks despite the cool of the night that followed her in from the landing like a swirl of cloak.

'Have you been out?' she asked.

He brushed water from his shoulder, aware of droplets at his feet. The sight filled his mind's eye, her car by the road, the grey shape of the man, their words masked by rain and distance. The motel, his imagination turning the walls invisible.

He flicked at his shoulder again, trying to dislodge the visuals. 'Only just got home.' He turned away, reached for a cup. 'So … how was it?'

He winced. Not the best way he could've framed it.

The percolator burbled as rain drummed on the roof.

A catch in her breath, then, 'Nothing special. I need a shower.'

'I'll be here.'

She crossed to him, touched his cheek. 'Won't be long.'

---

In the shower, she thought of the hotel carpet, a burnt orange with some black pattern as though someone had gone crazy shaking a fountain pen. A lamp, yellow and green, by the bed. The clunk of the Coke machine, and the way headlights sprayed across the print on the wall, some tropical beach sunset. The burr of semis. And while he slept, a siren that dug into her like a scalpel, filling her with dread. As if Charlie was outside, gone back on their deal, all fury and fists and fangs. That stupid scribbled note, as though she had felt the seed take hold, some moment of ignition. Of conception. And feeling so afraid. What the hell had she done? How would they survive this? How many secrets could a relationship hold? The click of the hotel door and the cold hit of the rain as she slouched to the car and sat behind the wheel, breathing deeply on a menthol that Charlie hated, part hoping he would follow, Victor, but glad to wipe away her tears and drive away when he didn't, the forbidden butt ground out in the ashtray as though marking her fall from grace.

———————

A week later, he suspected: some shift in her scent. A month later, she took the test. Her face was so alive, her heart hammering, skin flushed: you're going to be a daddy, Charlie.

'Great,' he said, happy for her, trying not to let his panic show.

# ROCK DEEP (VANCOUVER)

## 2001, SUMMER: VANCOUVER

She hadn't told her folks, her sister or even Ruby. It pretty much ate her up, not being able to tell them her big news as they had a farewell dinner at Maya's, waving a new job for Charlie and a music magazine internship for her as the reason for the move north. Charlie's connections, coming to the rescue, price unrevealed. Maya, sneaking her aside, saying how an old schoolfriend of hers — remember Victor? — had been asking after her, and she'd almost panicked — you didn't tell him anything, did you? — but it was just friends of friends, Maya said, giving her the sister look, about what it might be about and why now. A shrug, a mumbled 'dunno', hot cheeks, a flush going all the way to her groin. A 'hm' from her sister before heading back to dessert, glances over the jello.

It was, for all that it was scary, also good to leave Seattle.

The internship felt fragile, part-time as it was, a foot in the door that likely would get slammed on a young mother. Misgivings? You bet. But, there was this life inside her, a constant wonder, the desire for which continued to surprise her. She and Charlie finding an improbable purpose together.

Maya threatened to visit but it was as unlikely as her parents caring to, they never having owned a passport and Maya's one big overseas holiday being to Cancun for her honeymoon. Work and child would keep her pinned down.

So it was just the two of them as her belly ballooned, Charlie rapt in the sounds and movements of the baby, she nauseated but making do, worried about what to do when the baby came.

'It's not like you can drive me to the hospital,' she told Charlie.

'I can make it,' he said.

'Blood, Charlie. Lots of it.'

He shrugged, and she called Ruby, and then argued with Charlie, but by then she was a blimp and he couldn't deny her the help she needed.

At least he had the hospital covered. A favour that involved a trip to Montreal – he brought her back a magnet of a horse and cart that could've been from anywhere with old churches, Paris maybe – earned them a hospital room when the time came.

But it was Ruby who was with her in the cab as the contractions wracked her, and Ruby holding her hand when Layne made her appearance, no fuss, just after midday on a bright summer's day.

And Ruby, sitting by her hospital bed, having spent the nights on the sofa of their one-bedroom apartment with a view of a freight terminal and the harbour from the bathroom window but no elevator. Saying, 'I can see why you like him, Lee, but he's a weird one.'

'He has a thing with sunshine,' she said, aching and exhausted, and tired of defending him. 'A sensitivity.' Almost just letting it out and seeing what Ruby said. She was into horror stories; her art was all about miserable people and miserable places.

'No, I mean some of his stories. I love talking to him, especially about music, but, I mean, why does he need to lie? The other night he was telling me about seeing Led Zeppelin. He would've been in diapers, right?'

'Maybe he just got the dates wrong?'

'I looked it up on Yahoo! I don't think so.'

'He likes you. Maybe he was just trying to impress you.'

'Huh. He goes out all night, spends most of the day in his room, by the looks of it. How can you stand it?'

'It's how we get by, Roo.'

'As long as you're happy, I guess.' But she didn't sound convinced. 'It's just, sometimes the way he looks at me gives me the willies and the shivers at the same time.'

She imagined Charlie drinking from Ruby, Ruby clinging to him, eyelids fluttering, lips parted; she was too exhausted to worry about such fantasies.

'He's shy and nervous. He knows you're my best friend; he's worried you won't like him.'

'After how long? Don't worry about it, I shouldn't have mentioned it. You've got more important things to think about, Mommy. So how are you gonna get on when you get home?'

'We'll cope. Charlie will make a fine daddy. I'm more worried about what my family will think.'

And boy, she copped hell for not having let anyone know. Straw that broke the camel's back, her mom said, and what kind of damn fool name was that for a girl anyway? But Maya assured her she would come around. As long as she got to see her granddaughter before the kid was at school.

It wasn't long before she was wondering if any of them would last that long. Trying to be there for the baby, trying to keep the money coming in by waiting tables and writing for the magazine while Charlie worked the clubs, trying to keep Charlie from melting down because of this tiny new life that had him awed and petrified at the same time.

# WILL YOU BE THERE (IN THE MORNING)

## 2001, WINTER: VANCOUVER

He woke her when he slid into bed, his body a tepid hot-water bottle against her back. She felt like a zombie, exhausted by the routine of feeding and washing and worrying. Charlie worked seven nights, was barely functional during the day, treated Layne like she was a cross or holy water or something.

'How was work?'

'Same old.'

'Who was playing?'

'No one interesting.'

His breath, stale against her cheek; if he had a heartbeat, she couldn't feel it.

And because she was exhausted, she asked, 'Who were you with?'

'The usual.'

'I mean, who were you with, Charlie? You're warm.'

'You need everything you've got for the baby.'

'The baby drinks milk, Charlie. I understood while I was pregnant, but she's six months old.'

'Still,' he said.

She pushed him back as she sat up, uncomfortable against the bedhead. Could just make out his features in the hint of dawn edging the drapes, his eyes a dull reddish glow, his teeth white as a toothpaste commercial.

'You bored with me?'

'Of course not. I need you. You make me feel the best I've ever been.'

'But you don't touch me. Is it because of the baby?'

'Of course not. Only that you can't carry us both.' He took her hand. 'It's just blood, Corey. Just like getting Layne was just sex. A means to an end.'

'You know my mom won't talk to me because I wouldn't let her come stay after Layne arrived. Dad either. Maya's so pissed with me still.'

'They could hardly stay, could they? You can visit, soon as you feel up to it.'

'You aren't going to leave me, are you? Leave me stranded here?'

'Of course not! I love you. I just need a little more than you can give me right now.'

'Jesus.'

'What about you? Missing your family. I know what you've given up. Sex. Daylight. The beach. With me, at least. You think I'm not worried about coming home to find you gone? Back to Seattle, to someone who can be a regular husband, who can look after you properly.'

'None of that matters.'

His nostrils flared and she wondered what he was smelling. Some deeper truth she wasn't even aware of? Some hint she was lying? Their hands intertwined, clinging in the cold light of unsettling realities.

'Roy said—'

'Roy was a cunt.'

'True. But it doesn't change the fact I do need more than you can give me. I can't feed only off you. It's not enough, long term. But I can never love anyone the way I love you.'

'I love you, too. I miss you.'

'Okay,' he said, and she saw the change in his features, a sharpening, and held her breath as he reached for her.

Layne whined, then started to scream.

Charlie blinked, pulled back, looking almost ashamed as he turned, staring, as though he could see Layne through the wall. 'Nipple,' he said. 'Nappy not far behind.'

'Figures.' She dragged herself out of bed and wrapped herself in her dressing gown. Charlie followed her, to put the coffee on, his idea of helping. A means to an end, he'd said, and for the first time she was realising she hadn't really thought that through, just what the end would look like, and what it would cost her to get there. Her and Layne. The baby suckled, and Charlie made coffee he wouldn't drink.

# ROY: ON FEEDING

They were, for reasons not overly clear to Charlie, in Wyoming, and while Roy extolled the beauty of Yellowstone by night, though they had driven right past, the fact remained they couldn't eat bear. Which, in the absence of what Roy considered to be a safe bet, left them hungry and alone on a highway to bumfuck nowhere. Never, Roy said, a hitcher around when you need one, and roadkill wouldn't cut the mustard.

Charlie felt as though he had a grizzly in his guts, clawing to get out. He needed food, right the fuck now. When they pulled up for gas, he reached for Roy's arm.

Which was rapidly pulled away.

'Don't, Chuck; stop!'

Followed by a thump in the chest that put Charlie on his ass.

'We can't feed from each other.'

'Why not? It's just blood, right?'

'We're takers, Chuck, not givers. Hoarders. Not even symbiotic.'

'But we're still … human.'

Roy snorted. 'Jury's out on that. We take what we need, we process it, we discard the rest. There's nothing for each other once that's done. And without that, what is there?'

'So why did you do this to me?'

'I was lonely, Chuck. A moment of weakness. You ever travelled, Chuck? I mean, like, overseas? Really travelled. You can take in the sights, that's swell, but then it comes around to dinner time, and you're trying to work out the menu by yourself. Then you're at the bar, trying to catch an eye or make small talk. Then you're in your room, alone, hearing the world going about its business and it doesn't include you. You don't belong, you're just passing through. Gets you down after a while. Down enough that you say yes when you should've said no and wake up, well, in a bath tub.'

Charlie waited, wondering if more would come, some insight into Roy's progenitor, but the man shook the memory away like a retriever ridding itself of water.

'It's damn lonely in a crowd, Chuck, and we need crowds.'

'Company, you mean.'

'Food, mainly, but sure, company too, I guess. We're big fish, Chuck; we need a big pond, one we don't have to share.'

'But we're sharing.'

'Sure we are. But it's a good idea not to stretch the resources too thin, right. Keep a low profile. Last thing we want is to end up in prison. The very last thing we want. Especially if it's got a window.'

He snorted again, then waved the car keys.

'C'mon, Chuck, let's go get something to eat and find someplace where we can watch the world go by.'

# MY CRAZY HEAD

## 2002, SPRING: VANCOUVER

It was after ten when she got home, her feet killing her from standing all night. To think, she'd used to stand in queues, then stand in gig rooms and mosh all night, tossed around by strangers. Now a few hours of schmoozing at a record launch and she was beat, her breasts aching, and she didn't even have a bath to soak in, the apartment was that cruddy for all that they could grab a chicken and brie at Waazubee's. She was already ticking off the duties: something to eat to fill the hole the few canapes she'd snarfed down hadn't and to soak up the booze she'd a little too much of; feed the kid; bathe the kid if Charlie hadn't, which was likely; rock the kid to sleep; try to get a few hours before the kid needed feeding; wake up when Charlie got home in the early hours and hold out an arm in case he needed a snack; wait for the alarm to ring so she could shower and breakfast and express and do it all again.

She reminded herself, she had wanted this, even if moving to Vancouver hadn't been part of that plan. The smell of the kid's head, the love, the smell and feel of Charlie as he hugged her and kissed her before he left for work, the weight of him against her in the morning, the hot rush of his teeth and tongue on her, the languid sleep that followed. Talking to bands. Seeing her name in print. Getting paid, better than tips at diners, for sure.

She could hear Layne crying even before she had her key in the lock. God, Charlie, she whispered, and opened the door onto a dark room.

'Charlie?'

No answer.

Fear stirred, narrowing her vision as she tried to make out the details of the dark room, barely any street light penetrating the drapes, but a little greyness shed by the clock in the kitchen and the microwave display.

Layne cried again and she took a breath and turned on the light and blinked in the shock of it, but the room was as she had left it that morning. Poor little Layne, though, was safely ensconced on the change table, a clean nappy by her side, legs and arms thrusting at the ceiling like an overturned beetle.

Fear gave way to fury.

'What the fuck, Charlie?'

She flung her bag to the sofa and strode over to check the baby – fine. Just needed a change and a feed. Layne screeched louder at Corey's presence, as though sensing the meal pressing against her flesh.

'Little monster,' Corey said, hushing her. 'Where's your useless daddy, huh?'

She went to the bedroom and flicked on the light. Charlie was in the corner, hands around his knees as though his mother had sent him there, rocking slightly.

'Charlie, what's wrong with you? Layne was on the table. Anything could've happened. How long has she been there?'

He looked up, only just seeing her now.

'Charlie, what is it? What's wrong? You're scaring me, Charlie.'

'I … I can't be alone with her.'

'What?'

'She smells … so good. I can feel her heart beat. She's so small, so delicate. Corey, what if I hurt her?'

She stepped out of the room, clutching the baby, and changed her and fed her, and all the time Corey's hands were shaking, her breath jerking in her body, a sound like a freight train in her ears.

He didn't appear.

Only when the baby was under control, was mewling satisfied in the cot in the living room, did she go back in. Charlie hadn't moved.

'Are you telling me I should take Layne away?'

'No, I'd hate that. I can't believe how important she is to me. It's just, I'm so strong, Corey, and she's so delicate. And I'm so not … normal. I couldn't live with myself if I hurt her. I was there, changing her nappy, and suddenly, I just got the shakes. All I could see and smell was her. And I was frightened, really frightened.'

She kneeled in front of him and took his hands. Her legs protested, her knees ached on the thin carpet, the timber underneath pressing through her leggings, and in the back of her mind all she wanted was a hot shower and a glass of bourbon or maybe wine; there had been a Canadian red at the soiree that she hadn't minded. But she had a fire to put out and she made herself kneel and take his hands and keep her voice gentle.

'Charlie, you're her father. You're not going to hurt her. Just love her and protect her and be here when she needs you. I need you, Charlie. We both do.'

She led him out and made him hold their daughter. She felt her heart exploding at the sight of them together. She folded them both in her arms.

Crimson tears slipped down Charlie's cheeks. She took one on her fingertip and licked it, the metallic taint a jolt on her tongue.

'I've never seen you cry,' she said.

'I can't stand the thought of hurting either of you. I never thought I'd need anyone like this. I never thought I could. Not after … not after what Roy did to me.'

He nuzzled her neck, but she pulled away.

'You need to go to work, Charlie. And I need to sleep before this monster wakes up.'

He wiped at his face although the tears had already soaked into his skin; his eyes were bloodshot.

And when she got up in the morning, him beside her, baby gurgling happily in her crib, there was a tired arrangement of roses and a bottle of red wine on the table and a note, *I will love you till the day I die.*

She stroked a rose, the petal falling at the touch, and turned the wine to see the label: Californian. The note she stuck under a magnet on the fridge on her way to feed the baby. 'That's a long time, Charlie,' she whispered, and her voice sounded loud in the quiet of the room that smelled of sour milk and dying roses.

# TALL, DARK HANDSOME
# STRANGER



They were playing Scrabble, Layne sprawled on a rug nearby, when he broke the news.

'I've got to go back to Seattle. I need to renew my documentation.'

'There's no one here?'

'There's a guy in Gastown but I prefer to deal with the guys I know. Besides, I thought you might like to see your sister and Ruby?'

'Roo moved to New Orleans years ago. Helena got a job there.'

'I forgot that.'

'You and current events, Charlie.'

'Sands through the hourglass.'

'Okay, you're watching far too much daytime TV. We really do need to get out of Dodge. Well, the family will be happy to see us, but work won't like it. I'll need a few days to clear it.'

'No rush,' he said, sounding pensive, and lost the game by even more than usual.

Charlie drove. Corey stared out the window at the darkness, the world just the spray of headlights, the alternating glare of towns and shade of parkland. Layne gurgling in her chair on the back seat. Petrol station coffee. She'd driven this in the daylight, once, had enjoyed it despite the boy she'd been with, but now it was dark and she could barely see even stars.

As they neared downtown, it began to rain, and she felt a tear well as the familiar sights mounted. A glimpse of the Space Needle was almost too much for her. For a long while they drove around the same couple of blocks near the square, drizzle speckling the windscreen, turning the hustle of pedestrians into ghosts.

'It's not there,' he said, every time they passed the same section of street. A laundromat, a grocer's, a shuttered store covered in tags that might once have sold cell phones. Each time the panic in his voice rising, even worse than having to show his false ID at the border.

'You sure this is the right block?' she asked.

'Of course,' he snapped. 'I relied on it while you were — It's not something I'd forget.'

'Maybe it's closed.'

He pulled over, parking illegally. 'You take over. I need to walk it.'

The baby was crying. Great. She was gonna get wet. 'I'll park around the block. Don't want a ticket.'

She'd just got the diaper changed on a street next to a vacant lot with bright murals on the hoarding, aware of the smell of poop filling the cabin, when he found her, his hair slick in the street lights. Her back was saturated.

'It's a café now. The book store wasn't doing so well. Did you want to come in? Have a coffee?'

It was every bit as dull as she'd expected, Charlie disappearing out the back for an hour, coming back empty handed.

'A day, maybe two. They have it down to a fine art.'

'I have to be back at the magazine in three days.'

'No sweat.'

'I'm serious.'

'Yeah, no problem.'

His take on days, on time in general, was one of the things that irked her. 'Can we go to my sister's now?'

'We should get a room, don't you think?'

'Surely you could make it for a couple days.'

He was antsy, eyeing the customers, the staff, one leg jigging up and down.

He shook his head, barely hearing.

The waitress, aglitter with piercings, came over with the pot. 'Cute kid.' She fixed Charlie with her gaze. 'He yours?'

'Sure. Kind of.'

'She sure is,' Corey said, kicking him. 'Charlie's her daddy.'

'Lucky you.' She gave Corey the side eye as she topped them up, black liquid swirling in the white ceramic, the stale aroma flooding out. Hard to tell if the girl approved of her apparent cougar status.

'C'mon,' Corey said. 'I need a shower and something decent to eat, and this kid needs a bath.'

'I'm gonna stay for a bit,' Charlie said. 'Need to check a few things out. There's a hotel on John. I'll be there by morning.' He pushed a clip of bills at her.

'I thought we were getting a change of scenery.'

'We can drive around tomorrow night. And you can see your folks, right? They don't need to know I'm here. Just say you brought Layne for a visit.'

She could see it already, the takeout or the hotdog from a cart if she could find one this time of night, she munching through the dull food in front of the hotel TV while Charlie watched, half interested, his nose full of scents she couldn't smell, his eyes taking in things hers couldn't, turning his head at things she couldn't hear. Smiling at the baby he was scared to touch in case he broke her, or worse.

'Sure,' she said.

The hotel was little better than the café, in terms of scent and décor. She sorted the baby and showered quickly, came out pleasantly warm to find Layne crying for a feed and wished she could satisfy herself so easily. She rubbed gently at the invisible wounds on her veins. God, she needed a steak, washed down with a merlot. When she got back to Vancouver, she would get one of the girls from work and go out for a lush dinner at which they both ate and talked and drank.

She and Charlie needed to find a babysitter. They needed a night on the town, a club, a band, dancing. Fucking. Made her ache to think of it, but that was a step too far; it was all fingers and fangs with Charlie.

The hotel room pushed in on her, the beige walls and bright slash of the mass market painting and the white, hospital-tight sheets smelling of bleach.

'C'mon, kid,' she said, hoisting Layne onto her hip. 'I'll show you where mama got you.'

She wasn't sure where exactly she'd picked up Victor on that lonely road in the rain, but there was a late-night diner within spitting distance of the motel and she hauled the kid in there, suddenly famished, the smell of greasy grilled beef irresistible.

Layne was grizzling at being kept up past nap time in the unfamiliar high chair the waitress had brought and she was trying to shush her while she dabbed at the sauce dripping down her arm when a man stepped up to the table and said, 'It *is* you.'

# SECRET

2002: SEATTLE

Corey was taken aback, gaze jolting to that face etched in her memory, to her lap, to her daughter, back to his probing brown eyes, heat in her cheeks. Victor fucking Moreno. Of all the greasy spoons in all the towns in Washington …

'Excuse me?' she stammered, reaching for indignation, denial.

But he had already kneeled to the high chair and Layne. 'What's your name, young … man?' An eyebrow quirked as he took in the black jumpsuit. He looked up at Corey. 'I know pink and blue, but what's black for?'

'The night,' she offered.

'The night?'

'The one with the stars. We don't do the blue and pink thing.'

'Very sixties.' He looked back at the kid. 'Such … dark brown eyes.'

'This has been swell, Vic, but we have to go.' Flinching, aware she was channelling Charlie, almost summoning him.

'No, wait, please. I'd really like to talk to you.' He reached out, a hand on her arm.

She pulled back, stood, forcing him to find his feet as she started to pluck the bawling Layne from the chair. He stepped away, hands out.

'Please. I've … I've not stopped thinking of you.'

'I'm not in the mood for a high school reunion, Victor. And you're upsetting my daughter.'

The waitress hovered.

'C'mon,' he told Layne. 'Hush, it's okay.'

Amazingly, the kid settled into Corey's shoulder, her gaze on Victor as the grizzling eased to a bubble of slobber.

The waitress walked over. 'Everything okay?'

'We have to go,' Corey said.

'I'll get your check.' She stared at Victor, who ignored her.

'Please,' he said to Corey. 'Just a coffee. Finish your burger.'

The waitress paused.

Corey felt the cold splash of resignation, a pancake flip-flop that fired her to the night she'd seen Victor in the rain, and before that, her first sighting of Charlie in the club, that feeling of wheels not so much turning as breaking free of the hub and screeching off the road, leaving her in a sparking, crunching wreck unable to steer or brake, just hold on. She clutched Layne, gurgling, a fist at her mouth, but eyes on the stranger still, and Corey's stomach rumbled, and she surrendered. She eased Layne back into the chair and retook her own.

'You want anything then?' the waitress asked Victor.

'Coffee, please.' And then, as the waitress walked away, a hand on the chair opposite Corey's, 'May I?'

'Be my guest.'

She picked up her burger, aware of the sauce she'd smeared on her daughter in her haste, the patty tasting cold now and of cardboard. She put it down, wiped her hands, washed down the mouthful with coffee.

The waitress filled his cup, topped up hers. The diner was pretty empty; Corey doubted they'd get much time uninterrupted by their server. Maybe that was a good thing. He was solid; a tingle reminded her of the strength of him on top of her, and she felt herself flush again as memories flashed through her.

'That was a strange message you left,' he said.

'I thought it was pretty clear.' *Don't try to find me*, she'd written, full caps, amidst the desperate poetry, and yet, here they were, no apparent effort required.

'You're not that easy to forget.'

'C'mon, it was just a good night out.'

Aware of the waitress watching, hovering by the phone on the wall.

He looked pointedly at the child.

'Seems like it was more than that. That weird note … how did you know?'

She hadn't really, just, wishful thinking maybe? But knowing him, knowing it was Victor, not just some handsome stranger, she'd felt the need to … fuck, say *something*.

'Victor, I think we need to go now.'

'Do I get to know her name at least?'

'No.'

'I know you told me not to, but I did look for you for a bit. No one from school seemed to know where you were at. Your sister is very loyal.'

She shrugged, smiling, loving Maya, even as she felt her toes curling over the edge of a precipice, the risk of having picked up someone she knew now coming home to roost.

'And now here you are, the scene of the crime.'

'Crime?'

'Sorry. Where it happened.'

'Nothing happened.'

Layne gurgled as she threw a fry to the floor, and Victor bent to retrieve it.

'I beg to differ,' he said, placing the fry out of Layne's reach. 'Or am I mistaken?'

'The whole thing feels like a mistake. I really think we need to go.'

She straightened her jacket, looking for composure as she

tried to drive down the turmoil in her guts. The burger might be coming back. Great.

'Please,' he said. 'Can't we at least finish our coffee, talk about it?'

'There's nothing to talk about.'

'I think there's a hell of a lot to talk about.' He pointed to her hand, clasping the strap of her handbag, Charlie's ring glinting dully on her finger. 'Does he know?'

'It's really none of your business.'

'What if I want it to be?'

'That can't happen.'

'At least give me an explanation.'

She bent towards him, her grip on the bag tight, her knees threatening to betray her if she tried to stand. 'What is there to explain? I picked you up, we fucked, it was good—'

'It was better than good.'

'And that's it.'

'But it isn't. I deserve—'

'My thanks, and you got it ... several times.' Damn, that tremble in her voice.

Her gut lurched again as he pulled a badge from under his jacket and plonked it on the table and she swallowed back the rush of bile.

'I need to insist. Coffee. That's all.'

'Not with my kid.'

'Fine. How about here, tomorrow. One o'clock?'

'I ... I can do that.'

'You gonna stand me up?'

'How could I ... officer.'

---

She sat in the car, Layne kicking away in the baby seat behind her, and waited for her hands to stop shaking. She hadn't vomited, which was a plus, but other than that, she was in deep shit. She wished desperately she could drive to Ruby's and just blurt it all out – Charlie, Victor, everything – but Ruby had left town with her girlfriend years ago, and a phone call or IRC wouldn't cut it. She was really down to her mom and her sister in terms of significant women, and her mom wouldn't handle it and her sister ... Maya would freak. She couldn't tell them any of it. But perhaps Maya could babysit while she tried to dig herself out of this hole.

## UNDER THE SKY



Corey stood on her sister's porch, struggling to keep a grip on the squirming kid as she hit the bell. She was cutting it fine to get to the diner. What would Victor do if she didn't show? An APB? How hard would it be to find her? Her and Charlie? No way could that end well.

Her sister opened the door.

'Hey, Maya.'

'Corey! Why didn't tell me you were in town?' She tickled Layne's chin, making her squirm even harder.

'It's a bit last minute. Charlie had some stuff to do and I didn't know how long we'd be here.'

'You want to come in? The place is a mess, as usual.'

'I've got a meeting. Work, y'know? I was hoping you could …'

'Jesus, CeeCee, why didn't you ring?'

'I can take her to mom's, if it doesn't suit.'

'So where's Charlie?'

'He's got his own stuff going on.'

Maya stared at her, and Corey felt the flush. She used to be better at this. Maybe it was the mother hormones.

'Is everything all right, Core?'

'Sure, it's just, this trip came up suddenly, and then this chance to do this … this interview, out of the blue, and I could use the money. I mean, who can't, right?'

'You two are okay then? Are you gonna bring Charlie around? We'd love to see you both. All three of you.'

'We're fine, honest. I hate to do this, but, I'm kind of under the pump. So, can you?'

A squawk from inside the house.

'Sounds like Courtney would like to see her little cousin. Come here, Layney.' She gathered up Layne and the kit bag. 'CeeCee, don't be too late, hey. Come for dinner maybe?'

'Sure. I'll have to see how long this goes. Not too long, hopefully. It'd be nice to catch up. Sorry.' She kissed the kid goodbye and returned to her car. She paused at the door, looked around, Maya still on the porch, with Layne wrapped around one leg, watching her, Corey waving, then thinking, this must have been how Lot's wife felt, risking that one last look at how things had used to be.

Victor looked up from his wrist watch and caught her gaze as she opened the door, a buzzer announcing her arrival. Made her jump, and the door slammed behind her, making her jump again. She felt like a spy, about to betray her country: treason most high. But only Victor paid her any attention as she slouched across to the table, presumably anonymous behind her bulbous sunglasses.

She was ten minutes late, having been sitting in the car puffing back two cigarettes and squirting breath freshener before forcing herself to make the short walk inside. She wore jeans, Mary Janes, a t-shirt, puffer jacket and a beanie, no makeup: nondescript and undesirable. The gutter was yellow with leaves, the sidewalk slick with a recent shower; the chill cut through all her layers.

'Sorry,' she said, sliding into the chair opposite. Her hands were pale and veined with the cool, but she hadn't worn gloves, wanted him to see the ring she placed like a shield between them in her clasped hands after she'd folded away her glasses.

'Coffee? You look cold.'

'Sure.'

The waitress was on her like a seagull on a fry. 'Welcome back. You here for lunch?'

'Just the coffee. Please.'

She wrapped her hands around the mug, stared at the swirling black liquid, the ghost of steam, rather than at him, looking as he had yesterday in his dark suit and tight white shirt with a patch of smooth skin in the open V.

'I'm glad you came,' he said, his gaze like a heat lamp.

Interrogation?

She tried not to squirm. 'Don't. Please. I only came because you gave me no choice.'

'Sorry if you felt that way. I didn't mean to come across like an asshole. But I couldn't believe it, seeing you here. And with the baby.'

'She's one.'

'Right. Not a baby, I guess. Wow.'

She sipped. He kept his hands on the table, the manicured nails, long fingers on broad hands and corded wrists. She remembered those hands, moving over her, exploring her, holding her.

She sighed, the steam eddying, and she shivered as she gulped on the drink to try to calm herself.

'So where are you living these days?' he asked.

'You don't know?'

'I admire your faith in my abilities, but no, I haven't abused my position to search … whatever you think I could.'

'Thought you might have run my number.'

He glanced at the window, to the Chevy with its Canadian plates.

'Huh. Same car. I did think, back then, to put out an APB. Not that it would have done me much good, judging by those BC plates. When did you move to Canada?'

'In time to have the baby there. Their health cover's much better.'

'Anyway, I didn't abuse my position that way. Would've been kind of hard to explain, right? And yesterday, I was so rattled, so worried I'd scared you off with my assholery, I didn't even think to write it down.'

'You were rattled? My heart's still going way over the limit.'

'Guess I could book you for speeding. Take you in.'

She shook her head. Remembered him in the car, soaked, saying, 'you're the only good thing to happen to me today'. And outside the hotel: 'you sure you want to go in?'

'Hey.'

She jerked up, almost spilled the coffee.

'You okay?'

'Sure. Sorry. So, why am I here?'

He exhaled, long and slow, and she felt the weight on him, the hesitation. For someone who seemed so capable, so strong, it was fetching, and she felt that familiar slide, told herself, 'no', and pushed her thighs together, gripped the mug like a life ring.

He sipped his drink, barely touched, then looked up over the rim, catching her totally.

'So how long do I got you for?'

'Sorry?'

'How long are you here? In Seattle.'

'Couple of days. Just visiting. My husband's got business.'

'Not long.' He paused, stared at his coffee, out the window, then hooked her gaze again with those penetrating brown eyes that triggered something deep inside her. 'Do you want to blow this joint?'

'What? No. Where?' A hand to her hair, the constriction of her parka, the gaze of the waitress with the coffee pot at her elbow studying them like a raven trying to work out a puzzle. 'Sure.'

He threw a couple bills on the table and came around to take her chair and she was slow enough that he made it.

They paused at the door while he got his coat, a light splatter of droplets on the shoulders still.

'Where did you want to go?' she asked, breath fogging in front of her, arms crossed.

He paused, looking at her sideways, abashed, then she saw the decision cross his features as he faced her fully and pulled a fist from his coat pocket and opened it between their bodies so no one else could see: a key with a thick plastic tab.

'Oh, shit,' she whispered.

'We don't—'

'Okay,' she said, and slouched, hands in pockets, as they crossed the road at a jog to beat the traffic.

***

He opened the door for her. She paused, trying to remember the number, the grey light of the overcast afternoon conflicting with her memory of that rainy night.

'Recognise it?' he asked, on the lintel.

'They haven't even changed the carpet.'

'Lamp's new.'

'Smell isn't.'

She stepped in, slung her handbag on the table, hesitated, then removed her parka.

Victor hung his coat and jacket over the back of a chair. He took off the shoulder holster and gun and wrapped it in its straps and slipped it into a drawer beside the bed.

He walked to her, a hand on her cheek as she turned away.

'I haven't forgotten you. So strong, so scared. Lonely, kind of.'

'Sounds like you're describing yourself.'

'Yeah, I was pretty lost back then. Didn't even know where I was going that night, just walking.'

'Your knuckles …'

She took his hand, remembered the chaffed skin, how she had kissed the wounds, tasting blood and salt.

'I'd had a little trouble. Had to walk it off.'

A thumb on her lips. It tasted of gun oil, nicotine. She turned her head away.

'Hey, I brought something.' He retrieved his wallet, and she was ready to walk at the first sight of a condom, not the item itself – hell, yes – but the clumsiness of the delivery, the audacity, but he unfolded a sheet of well-worn note paper. 'Remember this?' Hotel letter head. Familiar script in thin ink.

'You kept it?'

'It was all I had.'

'Not my best work.'

He grinned. 'Your work was just fine.' He dropped the note, pulled her into him, his warmth leaching into her.

'There's something about you,' he mumbled, coffee breath blistering on her neck.

She stood statue-still, feeling herself slowly melting, a held breath leaking into the flesh by her lips, his scent of aftershave and tobacco invading the aroma of her fear.

'How long's it been?' His voice vibrated in her chest. Her nipples fired, a thrill running through to her groin.

'I don't need it.'

'Sure you don't.'

'Don't ...'

'C'mon.'

'This is a one-off,' she said, her hand in his. 'There's nothing happening here.'

He led her to the bed and guided her down and knelt with his hands cupping her hot, hot cheeks and then his lips were on hers and she surrendered, just like that, realising from the moment she'd seen him yesterday, maybe even from that night with him in her headlights, that this was always going to happen.

The tears came when she pulled up at Maya's. A yellow leaf fell to the windscreen from the skeletal tree and it triggered something. The smell of hotel soap unconvincing; surely she must reek of sex? Sex and the cigarettes they smoked after, during.

'You gonna leave me a note this time?'

Shaking her head, then, 'Her name's Layne.'

'Different.'

'As in Staley.'

'Ah.'

'You know him?'

'Of course. He died only this year. Big news.'

'Sad,' she said.

'That's drugs for you.'

'Oh, please.'

He held up his hands.

She saying, she couldn't do this again. A married woman, a mother, going back to Canada in only a day or two, a mistake. And he apologising, begging. Wanting to see her, to see *the* child, Layne Katarina, Katarina after her maternal grandmother, a concession grudgingly accepted by her mother. Just to have a moment.

Now, parked outside her sister's home, Layne inside, and Charlie likely asleep in the hotel room with its view of the apartment building next door. They couldn't leave till he had his papers, they had to do dinner with her sister that night and laugh off Charlie's unageing face, talking music and children and maybe politics if they wanted to go there. Knowing that tomorrow, while Charlie huddled out of the sun in the room they shared, she would be at the aquarium with their daughter and Layne's biological father, and after that, who knew? The tears came, and she wondered if her face would ever wash clean.

---

In the time it took him to buy Layne and her an ice cream, her butterflies settled. By the time they were standing beside the shark tank, she was allowing him to steer the stroller. There were no looks from passers-by, although a grey nurse seemed to stare and she moved them on to a tank whose residents had less-threatening teeth. Her mom rang when they were goggling at turtles and she allowed herself to be browbeaten into agreeing to dinner because she couldn't do lunch tomorrow because they might be leaving, depending on Charlie's business, and no, she didn't know if her interview, for a little magazine her mom wouldn't have heard of, would be published in Seattle. Victor checked his watch when she dropped her phone back in her handbag.

'You going back tomorrow?'

'Maybe.'

'Come back to mine, then?'

'What, with Layne?'

'Why not?'

'Vic … I don't think that's a good idea.'

'She'd not gonna rat me out, is she?'

'Jesus.'

'I was thinking about you all night. I couldn't wait to see you today. Please.'

She wanted to say, 'me too'. But all she said was 'sure', and found herself driving behind his car, Layne in the baby seat, wondering yet again what the hell she was doing.

By the time they got to his apartment, the kid was asleep, and mercifully stayed asleep for the time it took, a desperate but surprisingly tender moment on his couch while Layne slept on his bed with Corey's jacket for a blanket.

When she came out of the shower, he was tidily dressed and giving Layne a juice from her bag.

'I was gonna suggest we take the ferry tomorrow,' he said as she packed her stuff, making doubly sure nothing remained on the couch. She used the movement to place a pillow over a drying stain, her body throbbing in recognition.

'I don't think we can. This is it, Vic. Sorry.' And she was, feeling herself split into pieces again by a sudden tremor, relief and guilt and regret, jagged pieces digging into her lungs and guts.

He touched Layne's cheek, kissed hers. And at her car, a lingering kiss, a hand on her elbow reluctant to let go.

And then the aftershock, of Charlie, already awake when she got back to the motel under the overcast sky, telling her, he was sorry, he knew he'd promised only three days, but something had come up, he needed another couple. He'd have to go away, two nights, three max.

He stood, hands at his side, waiting for her anger, some argument about her lost work in Vancouver, the phone calls and excuses she'd have to make. But all she said was 'okay', already wondering what the weather would be like tomorrow, trying to remember when she last had taken the boat to Bainbridge.

# CRAZY ON YOU



They made the most of the sunshine on their last day to walk Discovery Park. The day before, he'd had time only for a long lunch, basking in a bright day to sit under an umbrella on the street. Today had been bliss, snacking under the trees, letting the heat melt into her while Victor chased a wobbling Layne in the shade. Corey had never been tanned but she'd never been this pale, either. Good thing about the Pacific Northwest, good thing about skin cancer: pale was in.

They grabbed an early takeaway dinner before retreating to Victor's. Layne wasn't wanting to settle and Corey's desire to be held by Victor was burning her, but she just couldn't let herself be too intimate with him in front of the child. Especially not with Charlie's imminent return.

God, she was a mess.

They sat on the couch with legs touching, a nightcap of bourbon at hand, with Layne scrambling around on the floor.

'I need to go. Charlie will be on his way.'

'Why?'

'Why what?'

'Why do you have to go?'

'Because I'm with Charlie.'

'You don't even know where he is or what he's been doing or who he's been doing it with.'

'You leave Charlie alone. He's—'

'It's not right, Corey. How he treats you.'

'You don't get to say that, Vic. What we do is our business.'

'You know how many times I've heard that? With the black eyes and the broken arms?'

'It's not like that.'

'So where is he these past three days? What's he been up to?'

'He does what he has to do.'

'I hear that a lot, too. In front of the judge.'

'Vic, you knew – we both knew – that this couldn't last.'

'Why can't it? We're good together. And Layne is my daughter.'

He seemed on the verge of tears and it was ripping her up, having to defend Charlie and herself. Herself especially. She should never have gone to the hotel with him, not that second time.

'I want to see you again,' he said.

'That's not a good idea.'

'I want to be a part of Layne's life. I want to be a father.'

'She has a father.'

'Who's where, exactly? I could be there for you both, every day.'

'There's no point to this game, Vic. You knew how it was.'

'And that's it? I get a couple days and then you're off back to your life in Vancouver?'

'You need to leave us alone, Vic.'

'How can I? She's my daughter.'

'It's how it has to be.'

He grabbed a tissue from the table and went to wipe Layne's nose, the kid intent on pushing blocks around, frowning at the intrusion.

Victor stayed kneeling, showing Layne how the bricks stacked while she showed him how easily they fell with a wave of a pudgy hand.

'You're good with her,' she said.

He gave a nod, as though she had just proved his point.

'You must've had a girlfriend. Someone serious. I mean, in school ...'

He shook his head. 'We were just kids, didn't know our ass from our elbow. You stood out, though. You and your girlfriend. I liked that you didn't take shit from anyone. Marched to your own beat.'

'And look at me now.'

'Looking pretty good to me, with this lovely daughter.'

'Yeah, I'm killing it.'

'You're a good mom. She's lucky to have you.'

He pushed a lock from the kid's forehead as she bulldozed another couple of blocks.

'Victor, you'll find someone else.'

He snorted. 'You make it sound easy.'

She held out a fist, thump up. 'You could try hitching.'

'Nah,' he said. 'You never know who's gonna pick you up,'

'That's the thrill of it.'

'As a responsible police officer, I have to advise against it, young lady.'

She smiled, he chuckled, crouched there beside Layne, seemingly unable to pull himself away. So unlike Charlie, who seemed almost afraid of the kid, or thought the kid was afraid of him. Animals, he'd told her once, didn't like his kind. Maybe it was true for children too.

'What were you doing, out there in the rain?'

'Walking.'

'Duh.'

He sank back, eyes on Layne, tissue poised as another droplet threatened to run free.

'Seriously, why were you out there, Vic?'

Silence, as he concentrated on wiping the kid's upper lip free, making her toss her head as he wiped at her nostrils.

'A fight? I remember your knuckles, they were pretty messed up.'

He looked at the back of his hand, tissue gripped there, then up at her. 'I'd punched a wall.'

'Resisting arrest?'

'Bad news. Not the best way to deal with it. So I went for a walk.'

'Out of the fire, eh.'

'Not at all.'

Layne crawled away from, leaving him looking bereft as she crawled into Corey's lap, a plastic block digging into her thigh.

She winced as she shuffled to accommodate the kid's weight, almost missed his mumbled line: 'Doctor had told me I had a cancer.'

'What? Oh, shit. You're better though, right?'

'It didn't kill me, obviously, but ...'

She cocked her head, dodging Layne's forehead as the kid blew bubbles, drove the block across her upper arm.

'But?'

He looked away, then back, a hand raised in her direction, in Layne's direction. 'It did take any chance I had of fathering a child. So I thought. And now ... this.'

'Shit,' she said.

'Yeah,' he said. 'Shit.'

The word hung there, just Layne's mumbling intruding into the silence as Corey thought again of the odds of meeting him on that night.

'You know, there are other ways to be a dad,' she offered eventually.

'But she's mine, Corey. Of me, I mean.'

'I know. But she's Charlie's daughter. I'm Charlie's wife, I love him.'

'And me?'

'I ... I've really treasured these days, Vic. You're a lovely guy, and if we'd met—'

'Don't. I don't want to hear that.' He shuffled through the minefield of blocks to take her hand. 'Promise me then, the next time you're in Seattle, you'll call me. You'll let me see you and Layne. Even if it's just lunch or a visit to the market. Promise me that much and I can live with this.'

She licked her lips, something inside fluttering. 'Maybe. Maybe we could do that. But that's all, Vic.'

'I'll take it. To let you go would be too much.' He stood, handed her glass to her. 'Let's drink to it.'

'To the last three days,' she said.

'To the next three,' he said.

They clinked glasses, a hollow desperate sound, and the bourbon did nothing to the cold ball of anxiety settled in her guts.

# THE WOLF



Corey was woken by the sound of the key in the door. She had made sure she was in by 10 that night, not having heard from Charlie. Sleep had taken a while to arrive, her mind dragging back to the what if – that night at the club, turning from Victor with his pals up the back to that lonely boy at the bar, and what if it hadn't been Charlie who had followed her out back with the douchebag …

'It's me,' Charlie said as she reached for her phone by the table, the motel clock radio unplugged to make way for the charger. Four in the morning. The world hushed. Layne squirming but not waking as Charlie padded past to check on her, then sat on the edge of the bed to strip, haul on pyjamas and slide his cold self under the blankets next to Corey.

He had to know. It would take seconds for him to smell the guilt leaking from her pores, surely. She and Victor, banging like co-eds at every chance, roaming Seattle like newlywed tourists, sharing their favourite eateries, living in a bubble with Charlie poised like a descending finger to pop it.

Stupid, stupid woman. Yet even now, with Charlie next to her, telling her he was sorry, her thoughts were on Victor, his incredible wonder and patience with Layne, and with her.

'Oh, hey,' Charlie said, leaning over the edge of the bed to rifle through his jeans. 'I got you something.'

She can just make it out, more by touch than sight. A magnet of the Golden Gate Bridge.

'You went to Frisco?'

'Only knew when we got there, but yeah.'

She sat up, rocking the bed. 'What the actual fuck?'

'I told you. A job.'

'And you couldn't take us?'

'No, the … the boss provided the transport. There was a group of us, in a van.'

She had an image of illegal immigrants squished into a truck.

'So what was the job?'

'I can't tell you.'

'Does she have a name?'

'What? No, it's nothing like that. I've always told you if I've had to … source my supply somewhere else. Like when you were pregnant, right? It was nothing like that.'

'Then what was it? The west coast vampire society AGM?'

'All I can tell you is that the papers I need, things like our move to Canada, they don't come cheap. I'm not rich, I don't have a big stockpile of antiques or art or anything, no property portfolio. So occasionally I have to do favours, okay? Back scratching. Harmless enough.'

'Jesus, Charlie, are you a criminal? Are you hurting people?'

She was trying to keep control but the anger, the fear, were filling her in a hot gush. Her voice was shaking with the suppressed emotion, Layne already gurgling, picking up on her distress. The image of Victor's badge filled her vision, his accusation about Charlie being some kind of criminal blaring like a siren.

She'd been expecting to have to lie or confess about her infidelity; instead, she was finding out her husband was a goddamn vampire mafioso. What the actual fuck indeed.

'It doesn't usually come to that. We turn up, maybe retrieve something, swap something, stand around looking like we mean business. Boring, mostly.'

She slipped out of the bed, glad of her pyjamas as his gaze roved across her; she slipped on her gown and belted it tight. She hushed Layne as she went to the kitchenette and poured herself a shot of bourbon, a flash memory of her and Victor last night. The bottle wouldn't be enough.

'Core, seriously, it's nothing. Low risk. Just business. Keeping us under the radar.'

'Just how many of you are there? How many van loads?'

He shrugged. 'We have to keep our distance. Keep moving.'

'Oh my god.'

'They think I'm crazy for being with you. For having Layne. They can't understand how I'd risk everything for you. I think they've forgotten what love is.'

'Everything?'

'Such as it is. I'm sorry I can't give you more, but I do love you, Corey. More than anything. Come to bed? It's been a long three days and I've missed you so much.'

She recognised the tremor in his voice. He was hungry. Hungry for her. She poured another shot and savoured the heat of the liquor burning down her throat, into the pit of her stomach. Victor was a dream, just a dream of a normal life.

She joined him on the bed, but held back, prolonging the duplicity, she guessed, the risk of discovery.

'What age is best, do you think?'

He paused, undoing shirt buttons, his chest pale and bare, unlike Victor's, matted and, by comparison, tanned. 'Hey?'

'To be frozen. Twenty? Charlie, I mean, look at you. No one respects a twenty-year-old unless maybe they're in uniform, and even then it's more, I dunno, pity? Twenty-five, you still don't really know what you're doing. Thirty, might be peaking physically, but you're really just starting to get your shit worked out. Forty? All the wisdom and not quite on the downhill slide just yet. I guess it's not so bad for guys, guys just go grey and get manly wrinkles. You can still fuck a woman when you're an old guy and get applause. Women, we just get frowned at. I'm already getting the eye for being with you, some kind of cradle snatcher. Have I already missed my chance at being my best immortal self?'

'I told you, the chances are slim.'

'You know what my chance is of being old and then dying? One hundred fucking per cent. But when do I call it? When do I take my shot? At what age do I decide to take my last breath … as a human, or at all? One more day of sunshine, Charlie. Another year with my kid not thinking I'm weird, afraid that she's gonna tell her teacher what her mommy gets up to at night, why her mommy can't do canteen, can't go to athletics, can't go to the pool.'

'You wanted to be a mom.'

'Don't.'

He shrugged, and she said, 'Do you wish you were older?'

'I'm plenty old.'

'But you don't look it. People treat you like you're not much more than a teenager.'

'I guess I don't really notice it. Never stayed still long enough for it to become a problem.'

'Boys,' she said. 'It really is a man's world.'

'A man's, man's, man's world,' he said, smiling, almost singing, then getting serious. 'You don't regret Layne, do you? All of that?'

'Of course not.' She bit her lip. 'She needs me.'

'I need you.'

'You need my blood. Anybody's blood.'

'No, it's more than that. You know it is. You're … you're wild, Corey. Wild and … and free. The way you walked into that club, the way you took down that dick … and you came back.'

She didn't feel wild, or free. There were lines around Victor's eyes, those scars on his chest – a knife wound from when he'd been a beat cop, she'd found out. Charlie, who she'd seen get stabbed, unblemished. Yeah, she'd come back, that kid with colour in her hair and a heart full of fuck you. But now, that girl seemed a lifetime ago, and she wasn't sure who was stepping in to replace her. And what about Charlie? He would be growing, changing too, right? The body might not, but the mind, the spirit, time would still affect that. He had to learn to use a cell phone, just like everyone else. (Except maybe her dad, who maintained they were making people lazy: 'just be on time'.)

They sat for a long moment, hands in laps, years' worth of questions rolling out in front of them.

'Jeez, Charlie, what are we gonna do?' She looked at the door, where on the other side Layne lay gurgling. 'What kind of family are we?'

He stroked her cheek. 'We'll work it out.'

She grabbed his hand, feeling the tears well. 'God, Charlie, you'll get to bury us both.'

'Until then, I get to love you both.'

He laid her down, unbuttoned her top, tugged down her pants, and she came quietly as he fed from her, and then tried not to cry.

# WHAT HE DON'T KNOW



She was late meeting Victor. The Seattle Center was flooded with people wielding banners and effigies urging the US to stay out of Iraq and it was impossible to find a park. She'd dropped Layne with her sister, who'd been reluctant to let her leave.

'It's gonna be chaos,' Maya had said, adding almost in the same breath how her husband said they were idiots and how Iraq should've been cleaned up back in the Gulf War.

Corey would've driven through downtown Baghdad to see Victor. A demonstration wouldn't put her off. But she hadn't expected so many. Thousands and thousands. It made her wonder, not for the first time, if writing about music and waiting tables made any difference to anyone at all.

Seeing Victor pull up made it all go away.

'No Layne?' he said, and the disappointment was crushing. 'I had to pull a bunch of strings to get the day off, I can tell you.'

'I want you to myself for just one day,' she said, and leaned across, unable to stop herself, suddenly desperate as the crashing cymbals and barping horns and pounding drums and defiant shouts echoed in the street. She kissed him long and hard until she ran out of breath, then told him, 'Take me home.'

That night, she and Charlie were at the Sit & Spin, a favourite, posters for poetry slams on the front window amid those for bands; she was knocking back a strawberry shortcake, trying not to think about her day with Victor, the guilt she felt picking up Layne from her curious sister who didn't seem to buy her 'quality time with Charlie' routine, the kid gurgling away happily enough in her stroller. She was distracting herself by telling Charlie of the time she saw Eddie Vedder here, how it wasn't unusual, how the band was being beat on for riding the grunge train and wasn't that crappy, how she never mastered Space Invaders, how she and Ruby had sat here talking of leaving their homes and squatting together and doing their laundry here, how she'd seen Mudhoney play here, how it was like all of Seattle rolled into one place, how Krist Novoselic had kissed her on the cheek once when a friend of a friend had said hi. She almost choked when, across the street, she sighted Victor with his collar pulled up and cap pulled low. It was almost as though he felt her eyes on him, because no sooner did she gasp, making Charlie ask if she was okay, than he ambled away.

The next day, at Pike Place Market, Layne in tow, they managed to find a table and get their order before her frustration got the better of her and she demanded to know what the hell he thought he was doing.

She was eating chowder, a fitting accompaniment to her anger and the overcast day.

'I can't believe he's so young,' Victor said, impervious to both the chill air and her anger.

'You didn't answer my question.'

'What's he got on you, Corey?'

'Got on me?' She gulped down a spoonful. She thought of Charlie's teeth in her, of the safety she felt in his arms; how he was good and kind and cared how she felt.

'He's only a kid.'

She almost snorted chowder out her nose. 'He really isn't.' And slurped coffee to try to hide it.

'Corey, I'm a cop, okay. If he's giving you any trouble …'

'He's not giving me trouble.'

'If he's got criminal connections, I can send him away for a long time. He won't bother you, I promise you that.'

'It's just … it's just that he needs me.'

'He's done quite a number on you, hasn't he.'

'It's not like that.'

'Then what is it like?'

'I love him. It's just … there are some things he can't do.'

'Such as?'

She waved her spoon, unable to answer that, regretting her words.

'Father a child? I guess that makes two of us, now.'

'It's complicated, Vic.'

'I get it. This can't be easy for you. I'm just not sure what you want.'

'I … I guess I'm not sure, either.'

'How long do you need? I want to be there for you. But you have to want to be there for me, too. I can't go through another one of these separations.'

Layne cried and he moved to comfort her, his meal untouched.

'You're good with her.'

'Big family. I've always wanted kids. Had given up … my folks will love her. Would love her. Would love you. I have two nieces, one older and one just fresh out of the oven, imagine that, they could grow up together.'

'Oh, Vic, that can't happen. We've been over this, like a goddamn cracked record.'

'So why are you here?'

'I like you.'

'Like.'

'A lot. I wish that was enough.'

He bounced Layne on his knee. His look told her it wasn't, but he could cope with it. For now.

She wondered what Victor would say if she told him the truth. Try to get her locked up? Try to stake Charlie out in the sun? What would Charlie say? That, she knew. His answer to everything: run and hide. Keep moving.

Too late, Charlie.

# BARRACUDA

2003: SEATTLE

She took a cab, ruing the money but needing some space. Today she'd had the morning at her sister's before catching up with Victor for lunch and a stroll in the U District where she'd picked up a neat jacket for a bargain. Then back to his place for early dinner and … dessert, but not in that order. A double helping. Tomorrow was her last day before heading north again; he had the whole day off but they had no plans, waiting on the weather to see what the three of them would get up to. Victor had picked her up around the block from Maya's, straight off shift, had been disappointed when she'd knocked back his offer to drive her back to Maya's. The smell of cigarettes, a golden oldies radio playing on the cab's radio, the creak of the seat, took her back to the gigs of her youth. Of Charlie's couch.

Charlie. Where was he? Hunting? Another boy or girl writhing under his lips, just to keep him going. Was Victor her version – just something to keep her going?

They'd argued, at Victor's apartment. The usual, in his bed, somehow moving from what to order for delivery to why she couldn't stay. Victor reminding her yet again he was a cop, that whatever Charlie had going, he could put a stop to. Could get him locked up. And her fear, naked and cold at the thought, driving her to get him to leave Charlie alone.

'Prison would be a death sentence,' she said.

'Men go to jail every day,' he said.

And she couldn't say, Charlie's not a man.

'You really care for him, don't you,' Victor said, and she said of course, he was very special to her.

'And me?'

'You're special, too.'

'We could go somewhere he would never find us, if that's what's worrying you.'

'He can find me. We're linked, him and me.'

'He doesn't even love you enough to marry you, ring or no ring.'

'That never mattered to us.'

'Well, what about now? Layne could use a proper family.'

'Proper? What does that even mean?'

'You know what it means. How long do you think you can keep this balancing act going?'

'You want out?'

'You know I don't. I want you and Layne with me.'

They'd made up, eaten, made up some more. He'd been happy at the thought of seeing Layne, a lingering kiss at his door as she promised she'd see him tomorrow as the headlights of the cab splashed across them. She hated herself for what she was doing to him, to both of them. Victor was right about the balancing act. How long could she keep it up as Layne grew older? She could feel the rope fraying under her feet. But she'd take Layne around tomorrow and take another couple steps above the void. And then go back to Charlie and that strange life they'd made for themselves.

She winced as she paid the cab and, head down, walked up to Maya's door and rang the bell.

'Coffee's on,' Maya said, eyeing the departing cab, a catch in her voice.

'Everything all right? How's the kid?'

'Watching TV with Courtney. Dave's just in the shower, he

won't be long. Come in the kitchen.' Then she whispered: 'He turned up just on sundown. I didn't know what to do.' A hand to her throat. 'God, he looks … he hasn't changed at all, Core!'

'What?'

A figure at the table turned to face her. 'Hey, baby,' Charlie said.

———

Charlie led her to the porch, Maya flashing concerned looks through the window as she fussed with the percolator.

'We've got trouble,' Charlie said, his grip almost painful on her forearm.

Here it comes, she thought, feeling the pit open up under her, no safety net in sight.

'There's a cop. He's onto us. Me.'

All she could say was, 'What?'

'I got a call. One of the guys here at the Underground. Someone asking around. I caught a cab over as soon as I hung up. It's not safe here, Core.'

'C'mon, Charlie, you can't be serious.'

God, it sounded so lame, but she was struggling to see, to breathe. Couldn't think where this was going. Remembering Charlie's strange absences, his 'favours' for mysterious others.

'He followed you,' Charlie said. 'He's still outside, parked on the other side of the street, a couple houses down.'

'What? Who?'

'The cop. Who else?'

Maya came out, mugs steaming on a tray. 'Everything okay, you two?'

'I don't know,' Charlie said. 'What do you think, Core?'

Corey grabbed a mug and sipped, wishing the hot liquid to thaw out her insides, give her some clarity.

'You want to tell me about it, Corey?' Charlie asked, ignoring the coffee.

'You're starting to worry me,' Maya said, putting down the tray. 'Should I get Dave out here?'

'No, it's under control. So, Core?'

She slumped over her mug, wishing she could just dive into it, like a portal, just slip away and reappear somewhere else, brighter and simpler.

'He's her father, isn't he?'

Maya almost choked.

'I can't have children,' he told her. 'Layne isn't mine. Not by birth.'

'Fuck,' she said.

Corey cracked, her sister's shock too much. 'He wasn't meant to know. I just kind of ran into him at this diner and he saw Layne and started asking questions. I just needed a chance to sit down with him and—'

'Was that your "school friend" you were with?' Maya asked. 'All these times you've dumped Layne with me?'

'Have you been taking Layne to see him too?' Charlie asked.

He was so calm about it. Maya looked fit to blow a gasket, but Charlie was ice. Of course he was.

'She is his kid.'

'That wasn't the deal, Corey. He'd never get to see her, you said. He wouldn't be part of our lives.'

'Okay,' Maya said. 'You guys obviously need to work some stuff out, but this isn't the time or place.'

'We need to go,' Charlie said. 'Back to Vancouver where he can't find us.'

'We need to talk about this with clear heads,' Corey said.

'We will. Once we're safe. Maya, do you have a knife you don't need any more? Something thick and sharp, like a carving knife. A screwdriver would do, I guess.'

Corey almost dropped her mug. 'What the fuck, Charlie? What are you gonna do?'

'Trust me. Both of you. Just give me a head start, and then pick me up around the block. Please.'

The guy was smoking in his beat-up Ford, looking patient as he eyed the house. The street was shaded with trees on this side. Charlie had to go a long way around to approach from the rear, sticking to the shadows as much as he could, and staying low, hoping he wouldn't be spotted in the rearview mirror. He hefted the shaft of the screwdriver, its tip white with crusted paint. Maya had grabbed it from the garage amid paint tins and a stained drop sheet from a reno they'd done when they bought the house. His vision narrowed as he crept forward, every footfall sounding like a bass drum. He could hear the man exhaling smoke, could hear the tobacco crackling under flame. He had no idea he was being stalked. A rush, a stab …

No evidence, Roy had told him. No bodies. Moderation. Caution in all things.

He reached the trunk of the car, the smell overwhelming, the oil and petrol, the rubber, the brakes. He almost hated to hurt it, but he had no choice. The guy knew where they were staying. He needed a head start and this was the only way.

He plunged the screwdriver into the rear tyre and jerked it out with a pop. He crossed to the driver's side and felt, more than saw, the alarmed eyes in the side mirror spot him as he plunged the tool into the tyre, to be rewarded with a gush of air and the quick flattening.

For a moment, he stood to his full height, the tool in his fist. The door opened, splashing light onto the footpath. The driver stepping out, reaching into his jacket.

Charlie ran, in a crouch, as fast as his legs could pump, waiting for the report, the impact. But nothing followed him but swearing as he rounded the corner and jumped into their car and told Corey to drive, Layne grizzling in the back seat.

# STAN: THE MOVEABLE FEAST

There was a guy, Stan, who he met at the Underground. The regular bartender, Teddy, gave him a quick shake of the head when he caught his eye, but Charlie already had his money on the table and chalk on his cue. He didn't mind Stan, for all that he wore fatigues and liked additives; he talked straight, if over the top, and played a mean game of pool.

It was Stan who told him what they had was a virus, some ancient thing probably dug out of some tomb that hooked into their DNA and made them something akin to but different to the rest of the homo sapiens.

Charlie had read folklore and fiction, watched movies, asked around, and it was all grins and shrugs, yesses, nos, maybes.

Roy would only ever say, We just are; always have been, always will be. Mankind's dirty little secret.

Stan, though, saw their kind everywhere. In Hollywood, on Wall Street, in the Pentagon.

Don't tell me the guv'ment don't know about us, he would say over the table, lining up his shot, hands unusually still while he contemplated the angles and force. Weren't for our vulnerabilities we'd be the best spies, the best soldiers, you could hope for.

I'm sure some of the young'uns have done their bit. I mean, it's not like we can have a day at the beach or somethin', but before the UV gets too much, we can be pretty useful, twenty-four seven, you mark my words. Especially these days, it's not so hard to throw your weight around and keep from gettin' sunburnt.

And later, over a jug of freshly squeezed, a foaming brew still warm but lacking that personal flavour, he'd inevitably opine that it was the soul they hungered for. Blood was well and good, but it was like the eucharist: it was more than just a liquid when taken straight from the vein. It was why over time just one donor wouldn't suffice. They ran out of soul, or the recipient built up a resistance to it. Was tapped out, either way.

Mark my words, he'd say. We need a moveable feast, a varied diet. And he'd point to the jug and say, This is ersatz. It'll get you through in a pinch, but end of the day, you need the real deal, the high octane, the soul food.

Stan liked jazz. That was another thing Charlie liked about him. But sometimes he'd hop the table with his theories, like, that HIV was a conspiracy by a vampire-hunting sect of the Catholic Church to destroy vampires but it had gone wrong and jumped to gen pop. God's wrath? Maybe. Charlie had never been one for God or gods, though his mom had been card carrying and his pa had gone along with it, certainly in so far as sparing the rod and spoiling the child went. All his mom's prayers didn't do squat. Maybe he'd had a death wish when he'd gone with Roy. Maybe. God's wrath or just his sense of humour? He'd never set foot in a church since. Had figured he was beyond saving.

And then he'd met Corey, who found him more than bearable if not redeemable. Everyone, Roy and Stan and her folks included, told them it couldn't work. But here they were. Making it work. Black ball, corner pocket. Bam.

# SWEET DARLIN'

## 2003: VANCOUVER

She was going over her questions numbered in her notebook when Victor rang. She almost didn't pick up. But she was in a cab – the office had given her a voucher because the band was doing interviews as their hotel, near Sea-Tac – and the driver wasn't chatty, playing reggae almost too loud for comfort, which was quite the achievement.

She told him he'd have to be quick, she was on an assignment, but she couldn't deny the buzz she felt from his voice in her ear.

She shouldn't have picked up.

When was she coming back, he wanted to know, but she had no plans. Maybe for Bumbershoot if she could swing it on the work tab. R.E.M. was headlining; had she told him about the time she waited on Michael Stipe?

'Your boyfriend still owes me for two tyres,' he said, throwing cold water on her reminiscences.

'You need to let that go.'

'I don't even know how he did that.'

'Told you, he's talented.'

'Must be for you to still be with him.'

'I can hang up.'

'Don't. Sorry.'

And then the mundane how are yous and how's work and what cases was he working, leading to the inevitable, 'I miss you', and her 'don't', questions about Layne and appeals for photos that she wouldn't send.

The hotel came into view through the windscreen.

'I have to go; I need the paycheck. Layne's had a cold.'

Was she all right? Was it serious? He could send money, he could be on the next plane.

She refused both. 'You can't come here, Vic. I mean it. I couldn't cope with that. You need to accept that we lead different lives.'

And found herself, as she reached into her handbag for the voucher, the cab slowing, promising to visit soon, before summer, sure. As she folded her phone away, her gut lurched when she realised she had drawn a heart around the number 3 on her list of questions, complete with an arrow through it.

---

Charlie felt as though they had a target on their backs. The cop had spooked him, for sure, and it had got to Corey, too. She'd been different since they'd got back from Seattle: tense, nervous. Every instinct was screaming at him to run further than Interstate-5, but he figured Corey was as far from her family as she was prepared to go.

There was no doubting it was tough, trying to raise Layne by themselves; tougher than they'd expected. Without the assistance of a cheap babysitter in the form of a kind elderly Chinese lady two doors down, they really would've been up against it. And he couldn't rid his mind of the hurdles to come, imagining the kid blurting out to her teacher the truth. Picturing the drawings being placed on the desk like tarot cards foretelling doom, a stern glance over glasses as a judgemental finger pointed out the red and black scribbles as a point of concern for the child's development. Is everything all right at home?

Everything was not right, the two of them fretting and alone, the kid soaking up every spare minute, every buck they could earn. He was trying to resist falling into the Underground, but the fact was, a trip south or east paid well when they needed it, even if it meant leaving Corey for a night or three to juggle her work at a café and the magazine on top of caring for Layne. He was gently surprised to get back from a trip or even a night of nightclub work to find her and Layne still there. She was feeling the call of family and friends, the familiar streets, but now there was a threat there, and his attack on the cop's car had further rocked her.

Being with him had been challenge enough, but now the risks and challenges had increased exponentially. She had chosen him over family, but now, with a child of her own, their life together surely had to be on borrowed time. At what point would going on without him be preferable to staying? If a suspicious cop wasn't enough to make her reconsider, it was only a matter of time before something else brought them to the crunch. Maybe this was his reminder of the thing that Roy had tried to warn him about, of what it meant to be human: living a life while waiting for the axe to fall.

# I WANT YOUR WORLD TO TURN

## 2003: SEATTLE

It was a bright, clear summer's day when they buried her mother. Corey's father had closed in even tighter, his hug fleeting and almost unnoticed, Maya his favourite and his rock still, the pair the centre of a vortex of mourners at church and cemetery. Some bloke from her father's men's club, who Corey never had liked for reasons she couldn't pin down, made an inane comment about how she had grown before trying to slobber a kiss on her cheek. She shamelessly used Layne as a shield and then an excuse to dodge the relatives and family friends she barely knew, content to hang with Ruby, who ran distraction like a pro linebacker, the two of them united as the black sheep, the ones who had left.

Charlie couldn't be at the funeral and his regret absolutely melted her as he railed at the weather and his own nature. As soon as the sun was down, he promised, he would be there, for the wake at her sister's house, and she wasn't looking forward to that, the empty chair where her mom usually sat, a glass of chardonnay at hand. Charlie couldn't be at the funeral but Victor was, at a distance, like some surveillance cop, and she wondered at the fact that the two men in her life couldn't be with her when she needed them most. For one anxious moment, she'd thought Victor was going to come over, elbow in amongst Ruby and the couple of hovering classmates and cousins, but he didn't, leaving her both relieved and bereft. If Ruby noticed him, she didn't say anything, not then or the next morning.

'He must be devastated,' Ruby said, responding to the lie about Charlie not being able to get off work in time for the funeral, her understanding a contrast to the unconcealed bitterness of the family that he let her go through it alone. Her love for him soared as she watched him shoulder that uncomplainingly after dark, when only the closest of friends and relatives remained, picking over the remnants of pastas, sandwiches and stale coffee. His stoicism made it all the worse the next day, dropping Ruby at the airport, secrets and shame barely contained, then at Victor's, fucking desperately while Layne lay asleep in Victor's spare room in a bed he had bought especially for her. He apologised again for not being able to be there for her properly the day before, wishing they could be together, yearning to be a full-time husband and father. Bearing up as she, yet again, said no; she would not leave her husband. They had a deal, and this was it. And when she left, he stood, arms up against the door jamb like a man hanging on for dear life.

# RAGE

## 2005, AUGUST: VANCOUVER

Going in to the office made her feel like an imposter. It was on the second storey of a stained concrete building with dodgy heating, just able to call itself downtown, and staffed by eager young things or older musicians still striving for that hit in their spare time. They called her Seattle except for the magazine's editor who called her Grunge when she came in a day a week to write up her reviews and interviews, a fan girl working for beer money. But she loved it; it made her feel part of something, even if that something felt like a world away from sneaking into the Off Ramp when Seattle was the centre of the universe.

She was sitting at the desk she shared with the other stringers, her earphones in, struggling to hear the words of the bassist she'd interviewed two days before over the clash of cutlery and music in the café where they'd met to publicise an upcoming gig, a no-name local act in a small-name venue but something going on in their post-punk revival shtick (note: do not mention the resonance with Joy Division; they hate it).

She was slow to register someone mention her name – her actual name – and looked up belatedly to see the receptionist, she of the three-shades-of-orange hair (this week) and the nose piercing, pointing vaguely in her direction and Victor already striding past the desk, making a bee line for her. Serious look. Detective mode.

She fumbled to turn off the voice recorder, was still reaching for the ear buds when he loomed over her. His shoulders were squared under his mac and he had that focus: like he was on a case, a bad one. He clutched a manila folder protectively under one arm. His free hand wiped the rain-wet fringe from his forehead, his spiky hair reminding her of an alsatian with its hackles up.

'Hey,' he said.

'What the hell are you doing here?'

'You don't sound happy to see me.'

'I'm just shocked.'

'Hardly a secret.' He dropped a curled copy of the magazine onto her desk.

'It's not like I've got a reason to hide,' she said.

'Maybe you should have.' He laid the folder down on top of the magazine.

People were staring across the desk dividers. The editor was standing up, peering through the glass partition that walled off his office. He had a phone in his hand but hadn't dialled, she didn't think.

Victor tapped the folder, drawing her attention back to it. His cologne wrapped around her, adding to the fug of confusion his presence had conjured. Two worlds colliding, and she was suffocating.

'I need to show you something,' he said, and flipped open the folder. 'Recognise this guy?'

Charlie's face stared up at her, black and white squares: contact prints. Passport photos.

'Should I? Oh. Of course, maybe. It looks like Charlie.' The photos filled her vision; youthful Charlie, unchanging Charlie, Victor's finger pointing like a sword of Damocles, and her gut falling through the chair as the cold fear washed over her.

'Found these in a forger's back in Seattle. Citizen phoned it in after seeing an Arab go into a back room at a café. Thought it might have been Al-Qaeda.'

His stare penetrated her, right to her spine, but his words were coming in from a distance, as though she still had the earbuds in.

'I thought they looked like Charlie,' he said. 'But I guess they can't be, because this folder goes back to the 1970s. He'd be in his forties or fifties by now, right.'

'Right,' she mumbled. 'A crazy resemblance.'

'Resemblance? He's the spitting fucking image.'

'I don't know what you're asking me, Vic. You just said it can't be Charlie. So it isn't. A coincidence. Charlie certainly isn't Al-Qaeda or anything like that. He's nothing like that.'

'Sure. Just a coincidence, like you said.'

She closed the folder, pushed it away so she could stand up. She gathered some things from her desk into her handbag and slung it.

'I don't know what this is about, Vic, but this is not the place.'

She looked around, and his gaze followed, her workmates like prairie dogs dodging their glances; her editor, at his doorway, studying them.

'I have to go pick up Layne from daycare,' she lied.

'I busted my balls to get here,' he said.

'I still don't see what this has got to do with Charlie and me. Or you. I thought you were in armed robbery.'

'They've called a lot of us in. There was some weird club in the basement. Real kinky shit, apparently. Fingers in all sorts of pies.'

'I really have to go. They charge me extra if I'm late.'

'I'll walk you out. I can drive you, if you like.'

The editor asked if she was all right as they walked past, and she fobbed him off, an old friend from Seattle, grabbing a coffee, she'd file her piece in plenty of time.

On the way to the elevator, which took a lifetime to arrive, she told Victor, 'My car's here. Besides, shouldn't you be getting back to Seattle? Checking out the kinky shit.'

'I'm on duty. Following a lead.'

'You're way out of your jurisdiction.'

'You can't brush this under the carpet, Corey. You need to talk to me, before the shit hits the fan.'

In the elevator, going down, he seemed almost ready to cry. 'I wish you'd talk to me.'

'Victor, I can't. You shouldn't have come.'

At the front door, as she flipped up the hood of her jacket, and he told her not to leave him this way, begged her to talk to him, she said she'd call him, and they went their ways, he to his rental and she to her car. She sat at the wheel, rain on the roof, on the windscreen, as she got her breathing under control. She fumbled for a cigarette and breathed it in. She checked the time. Charlie would still be asleep, probably, although it was dull day, maybe he'd be awake. Didn't matter. What hadn't Victor told her? Why had he rattled her tree like that? Some kind of power play? Tired of sharing, finally? All his snooping finally paying a dividend. She cursed herself for all the clues she'd given him. Finding her wouldn't have been a problem at all, not for Victor.

She sniffed, wiped her face, started the car, hit the wipers. Layne first, then Charlie. Pronto.

----

She fumbled the keys as she balanced Layne, the two of them damp from the run from the car to the door, and her arms and back burning with Layne's weight after the jog up the stairs, too impatient to take the elevator the two flights.

No higher, Charlie always said when looking for a place. I need to be able to jump if I need to. He was afraid of fire, afraid of being trapped. Always had to have a fire escape, or at least more than one exit.

She nudged the door shut with her boot, didn't hear it click, didn't care as she put Layne down, relieved to be rid of the weight. There weren't staying long. 'Charlie!'

'Here!' From the back room. Thank goodness he was awake. She rifled the desk for their IDs. Had Victor found copies or something incriminating at the Underground? Is that what he was telling her? Giving her a chance to get away, torn between love and duty? God, she loved him, but she barely understood him. Either of them.

She was being torn down the middle, right now, and it was only Layne holding her together as the kid sat on the sofa with Mr Teddy, making whooshing noises.

'Charlie, we got a problem. The cops have raided the café – the Underground. We have to get out of here.'

He stood at the door in just a t-shirt and boxers, his face waxen, eyes shadowed.

'I got a call. We should have time. They got a tip-off, got everyone out before the cops arrived. Friends in high places, I guess.'

'No, we really need to get moving, Charlie. They've found your old photos. They're on to us.'

He swore, glanced at the curtained window. 'I can't go out,' he said. 'I haven't eaten in days. I need the night, Corey.'

'It's raining,' she said.

'Doesn't matter. It's like acid out there at the moment.'

She looked at the papers in her hand, at Layne playing happily. She thrust the passports and the wad of emergency cash into her handbag, then pushed him back into the bedroom and kicked the door closed.

'Be quick,' she said, pushing up her sleeve. 'Not too much, just what you need for us to get out of here.'

'Is it that bad?'

'Vic came to my work. Giving me a head start. That's all. He's a good cop, Charlie. He won't be far behind.'

She let him pull her to the bed and sat on the edge as he kneeled, her arm in his cold hands. He licked the inside of her elbow, a familiar shiver seizing her as his soft tongue gave way to the sharp penetration of his teeth, and then the gentle sucking as he drew her blood. She sighed, heard something, just enough warning to look up through her bliss to see the door opening and the space fill with Victor, his gun in his hand, and the shock on his face as he said, 'What the fuck?'

And then, 'Get the fuck away from her!'

He charged in, got a hand to Charlie's collar and jerked him away, threw him into the wall with enough force that a photograph of the three of them tumbled from the bedside table and smashed on the floor.

'No, Vic,' she shouted.

'What the hell has this freak done to you?' He jerked her to her feet, a hand clamped to her wrist, the other pointing the pistol at Charlie, squirming on the floor. 'You're bleeding!'

'You don't understand. Charlie's not like us. He's—'

Charlie sprang, holding the gun up in the air, his other hand at Vic's throat, driving him back. Corey stumbled and pulled free as Victor fought for purchase. The back of Victor's knee caught the corner of the bed and the two men toppled. She ran around to see them grappling on the floor.

'Stop, stop it, the two of you. Stop this!'

But they wrestled and swore and tore at each other, and then the gun went off and they lay still as the report echoed around the room.

Layne's crying penetrated the hum in her ears as Victor slowly got to his feet, one swollen eye already starting to close.

'Jesus,' he said. 'Corey, I'm sorry, I didn't mean for this to happen.' He kneeled beside Charlie and felt for a pulse.

'Don't do that. He'll be fine. I think. God, I hope so. You need to go, Vic.'

'Corey, I shot him in the chest at point blank. I can't feel a heart beat. I'm so sorry it happened this way.' He holstered his weapon and pulled a cell phone from a belt pouch. 'I need to call an ambulance.'

She snatched the phone and backed into the living room.

'Corey!' He stood, hands on hips. 'He's been shot, for God's sake!'

Layne was standing near the bedroom door, crying, the bear dangling from one limp hand. Corey grabbed her spare hand on the way past, pulling her gently but firmly with her.

'Charlie?' Layne said. 'Dad?'

'No, Layney,' Victor said. 'She shouldn't be seeing this.' He followed Corey out and pulled the door shut. 'Please, give me my phone. Or at least ring 911.'

Corey hustled Layne behind her.

'You need to get out of here, Vic. I mean it.'

'You know I can't do that.'

The walls crashed in on her, her chest tight, vision seeing nothing more than that last glimpse of Charlie's feet through the doorway, her ears filled with her daughter's crying.

'This is insane. You're both insane. I have to get Layne out of here.' She sat the child on the sofa so she could collect their things.

'Wait,' Victor said. 'Corey, we can work this out. Just let me call help.'

He crossed to the phone on the kitchen wall, but she ran up beside him and yanked the cord from the socket.

'No phone calls, Vic. He'll be all right. You need to get the hell out of here, and I need to get Layne away from this. Don't try to stop me, Vic. And don't you dare try to find me. Not till I'm good and ready.' It was something she kept telling him, she realised. Maybe this time she meant it. She reached for the door, pulled herself back to stare at the bedroom door. 'Oh, Jesus, Charlie. I'm so sorry.'

Sobbing, she grabbed her bag and bundled up her daughter.

Victor reached for her, tried to bar her, and she swore at him.

'What are you going to do, Vic? Shoot me too?'

And he stood back.

'If you know what's good for you, you'll get out of here and forget all about us. I mean it, Vic.'

She ran, this time not feeling the pain or the weight as she clutched her child to her, raced down the stairs. She ignored the rain and got them on the road. The wipers worked overtime and Layne cried for Charlie and Mr Bear, and Corey's vision was bleary with tears, and all she could say was, oh Charlie.

Should she have stayed? Tried to get him to safety? No doubt someone had heard the fight, the shot. Surely the police would be on their way. And what if they found Charlie and did an autopsy? Or if he was okay and they took him to jail. That would really open a can of worms. But she was on the road now, and Victor had just stood there, not hearing her, not listening, not helping. No way would he have helped her try to cover up the shooting. He'd go to jail first.

Where had he shot Charlie? Not in the head, she didn't think; the chest maybe. She told Layne everything would be all right, not believing it for a second as she remembered Charlie telling her, don't hurt my heart, Corey, my heart's fragile.

# NOBODY HOME



His chest hurt like a mother fucker. Someone had taken a poker and heated it up till it was white hot and then rammed it between his ribs. The stench of gunpowder was overpowering, his hearing was still dampened; he had a pretty good idea he'd been on the wrong end of Victor's gun. He reefed open the bedroom door, just as Corey was slamming the front door. Getting Layne away. Good.

'Let her go,' Charlie said, and Victor whirled, fumbling his draw but the gun finding Charlie's centre of mass on reflex.

'Fucking don't shoot me again, it fucking hurts.' Charlie put his hands up, aware of the black-rimmed hole in his white tee, the faint vestiges of blood, just below his sternum.

'What the hell?' Victor said.

'Just put it down. She'll be back when she's calmed down.' The wound felt like it was filled with maggots, chowing down as the flesh healed. But he was running on empty, his vision dark, muscles rubbery.

'I shot you. There were no life signs.'

'There usually aren't. Hey, Victor. There's something you've got that I need.'

He was close enough and fast enough to bat the gun from

Victor's grip, and then he socked him hard on the jaw, and when the man slumped to the carpet, he followed him down, pushed his head to one side, and without ceremony opened his throat.

It was almost sundown when Victor came around. Charlie had taken the policeman's car, managed to get him into the back seat and away before any heat arrived. Maybe the neighbours didn't care, were used to loud bangs in the area. Now they were in a derelict bar he knew, Victor moaning on a tatty pool table in the light of a couple candles Charlie kept here in his emergency pack tucked into a hidey hole in the ceiling in the restroom.

Victor rubbed his head, his throat, gingerly, and his fingers recoiled when they found the plaster on his neck.

'What the hell?'

'I needed it to undo the damage you did. I figure we're even.'

'The hell you say.' He levered himself up, sitting on the cushion, legs dangling.

Charlie, in clean clothes, his trench coat draped to the floor, straddled a stool. He had taken a second helping here, making up for the radiant sunburn, had managed to stay awake until the soporific sun outside had released its hold.

'Don't worry,' he told the cop. 'The wound will be gone in a day or two. You won't have to worry about your colleagues making fun of your hickey.'

'You better start talking.'

'Roy told me our saliva's a funny thing: part anaesthetic, part anticoagulant. But when the blood's in our mouths, it kind of … metabolises or something. Helps the wound heal. Keeps the herd happy, is how he put it. He obviously never met Corey.'

'You're still not making sense.'

He stood slowly, his eyes taking in the ruined pub, his gun by Charlie's elbow on the bar.

'Where are we, anyway?'

'A place I know. Take a seat.' Charlie pointed with his foot to a nearby chair, its cobwebbed legs pointing to the ceiling from where it sat on a dusty wooden table. 'Corey won't be back any time soon. She was really steamed, but I guess it was always gonna come down to this. You and me.'

'I guess.' He tapped his pants pockets either side of a stain on his pants front, frowned at Charlie, then sat. Dug a crushed cigarette packet from his coat and tapped one out, then found his matches.

'I really don't like the smoke,' Charlie said, 'but it's been a day. Go ahead.'

Victor lit up and breathed in a long stream, winced, breathed out real slow.

'You want to tell me what this is all about?' he said.

'What do you think this is all about?'

'It can't be what it looks like, that's for sure.'

'Is that what Sherlock Holmes would say?'

'What the fuck's that got to do with it?'

'Occam's razor and all that.'

'I'm more worried about Corey and Layne than playing pretend detective.'

'She can take care of herself.'

'Maybe, maybe not. That was some weird shit we found in Seattle, and you're clearly in it up to your neck.'

Charlie laughed.

'This isn't a joke, pal.'

'Fine. I reckon I know where's she's headed.'

'Okay than, we'll do it your way for now. But we gotta go past my hotel. I need to get myself cleaned up.'

Charlie eyeballed the blood on his collar, the mess in his crotch. 'Good idea.' He stood and tucked the gun into his waistband. 'But I'll keep a hold of this for now, okay.'

It rained all the way to Seattle. Maya looked stunned when she opened the door to find the pair of them on the porch.

'Charlie? What are you doing here at this time of night? Is everything all right? Where's Corey?'

'She's not here?'

'No, I haven't heard from her. What's all this about?'

'She's fine, honest. You know Victor?'

'That Victor? Well. This is a turn-up for the books, isn't it. This is something.'

'Oh, it's something, all right,' Victor said.

'You want to come in?'

Courtney called from the back room and she told her just a minute, mommy was busy.

'Maybe Roo's, then,' Charlie said. 'That feels about right.'

'Oh, I wouldn't think so,' Maya said. 'Not with the storm and all.'

'You got her number, Maya? An address, maybe?'

'I think so. Sure. Just a minute.'

She came back with a piece of paper. 'But the weather's saying it's not looking good. They're telling people to get out. She wouldn't go there, would she? Not with Layne. Not if there was danger.'

'She might if it was the lesser of the two evils,' Charlie said.

'She just might,' Victor said.

After offering reassurances and saying their goodbyes, they headed back to the car.

'You know my boys will be looking for me when I don't show up?' Victor said as they stood by the vehicle. 'How far do you think you'll get?'

'Far enough, with your help. You do want to help Corey, don't you? Be a good daddy?'

'Don't push me, pal.'

'Then buckle up and hope your buddies don't get in our way. Because I love her, Victor, and I will do anything for her. How about you?'

'Just give me the keys, freak.'

'You know, Victor, I figure it'll take us maybe two days'

straight driving to get to New Orleans. You might want to think a bit more about how we're going to get along.'

'Whatever. Are we going or having a pissing contest?'

Charlie snapped his hand around the keys. 'I'll take the night shift, Victor. You should get some sleep. We've got a lot of road to cover.'

# WHEELS

2005: ON THE ROAD

Victor smelled of body odour and greasy food and stale coffee, leaning against the car, finishing another gas station corn dog before taking the keys. Crunch time, even though Charlie had kept the pistol. Victor would literally be in the driver's seat till sundown. Anything could happen.

'I guess there'll be some explaining to do, back in Vancouver,' Charlie said as Victor licked the stick clean.

'Nah, there's no evidence of anything.' He wiped his mouth, his hands, dumped napkin and the tiny stake in a nearby bin. 'You think she'll be happy to see us?'

Charlie shrugged. It didn't matter what she wanted. Not with the storm coming.

'I knew her in high school, you know,' Victor said, and Charlie felt his hackles rise as the pissing contest recommenced. 'She was special, even then.'

'The odd one out that everyone wanted to squash into a box?'

'No. Not me.'

Charlie raised an eyebrow, unable to hide his cynicism. 'Emilio Estevez to her Ally Sheedy?'

'You know that movie?'

'Nights are long. What else is there to do if you're not at a gig?'

'Huh. I wouldn't want to change her. I wouldn't want her to change.'

He enjoyed Victor's apparent surprise that he could enjoy human entertainment, that maybe he wasn't entirely the monster the cop had thought. 'That always pissed me off,' he said, driving the point. 'That Ally had to change to be accepted.'

Victor grunted again. 'So what's the plan? Eenie meenie miney moe? Rock paper scissors? Pin the tail on the fucking donkey?'

'That'll be for the three of us to work out, what's best. Best for Corey, best for Layne.'

'Well, look at us, getting along.'

Charlie handed over the keys.

---

Charlie was surprised to have made it this far. It had nothing to do with the road blocks and traffic flowing out of New Orleans, and everything to do with Victor getting to drive all day while Charlie huddled under a blanket on the back seat. He was used to being itinerant, but never this vulnerable, and he slept fitfully and hungrily in the August heat as they worked their way to the Gulf.

'This is madness,' Victor said. 'What makes you so sure she came this way, through all of this? The storm's already hit Florida and they're saying it's swinging back.'

'She's resourceful, and we've been together for a decade. I can find her as surely as a trout can swim upstream.'

'Swimming might be just the thing if Katrina hits bang on. But I've got nothing else to go on, so all right. But we're in the shit now, pal.'

They had pulled off the road to refuel from a jerry can bought back in Amarillo when the radio gave them inklings of how desperate the situation was in the south, in between golden oldies and ads for crap.

The biting stench of the fuel made Charlie snort. He'd loved it once, a clear sign of freedom, but now it clung and spoke only of headlights and dead bugs and semis and road kill and he was done with it. Geography by night wasn't that much fun when defined by white lines and reflectors. They needed to get Corey and Layne to safety and sort this mess out.

He squinted in the late afternoon sunlight, taking in the strength of the muscles in the cop's neck and shoulders, the empty holster at his belt. The comparative tan.

It would be an interesting conversation between the three of them. Sunburn was nothing compared to his fear of how that would go. He couldn't believe how quickly he had come to need her, even after her blood had started to lose its potency. The thought of losing her … yeah, the sun had nothing on that.

Victor removed the can and funnel. 'Hope we don't have to get too far once we get a hold of her. We're starting to cut it fine.'

'It's not far now. It'll be getting away from the storm that'll be the thing.'

'Katrina or Corey?'

'Both. No point in putting it off.'

'Still won't give me the address, huh?'

'Give me the keys. I can take it from here.'

'Sun's up.'

'I can make it.'

'Roads are pretty risky, too.'

'Flash your badge. Or I can try to convince them to let us through.'

'No one needs to get hurt.'

'And they won't, unless they get in the way.'

After a moment, Victor threw him the keys. 'Fair enough then.'

# ANYTHING IS POSSIBLE

## 2005: NEW ORLEANS

Corey stood by the kitchen window in Helena and Ruby's house, hugging a coffee as she looked out past the big tree in the backyard, Ruby's workshop, the fence between them and the London Avenue Canal levee.

Ruby's wife was pulling a double at Charity. 'She wants me to leave, back to Seattle or her brother's in North Carolina, but I can't go when she's here. Besides, this is her parents' house and their parents', and it's never taken so much as a drop, not even during Andrew. We'll be okay here. But if you want to get out, I understand. If it hits us like they're saying it might, the town's gonna take some time to recover, for sure. It might not be a good thing to put Layne through.'

'No, it's okay, she's old enough now. We've got water and batteries for the radio, the windows are all taped up, and I'm here with you and, to be honest, Roo, I really don't got nowhere else to go just now. We'll ride it out together, and then I'll work out what to do next.'

Corey had been able to tell Ruby only so much, about how Charlie wasn't Layne's birth dad, which Ruby said explained a little about his attitude, which Corey didn't press her on; and how the two men had met and it hadn't gone well and she'd panicked and hit the road rather than weather the testosterone storm. She'd take Katrina any day.

Victor had rung, and Charlie had rung, and her sister had rung to say the two of them had been there and might be headed her way, but she figured the storm would have to give her some extra time. At least Charlie was alive, and it had taken all her strength to not jump in the car and drive back to him, but there would be Victor, and what if there was another gun shot? They were putting her in an impossible situation, one where she simply couldn't work out the right answer for them or herself.

'Is it really so bad, you'd rather sit through a hurricane?' Ruby asked.

'Either way, I'm the meat in a sandwich. At least this is one sandwich I can choose.'

'A po'boy. You're the meat in a po'boy.' She laughed and they hugged. 'Let's have lunch, then. If it does hit us, we should have a good view from the top floor.'

'God, Roo, you are such a Goth.'

'As Goth as fuck, baby. You want salami on your sandwich?'

---

It was late Sunday afternoon and the city was quiet and hot, not even dogs barking, and the women sat in the kitchen with the radio while Layne played on the floor with blocks. The rattle of wood on timber was the loudest thing in the world as the kid knocked them down, rebuilt them and knocked them down again.

'Curfew,' Ruby said, checking the clock on the wall. 'It'll be dark before long. Still glad you stayed?'

'Of course.' She reached across to squeeze her friend's hand.

'You know you can tell me about it. No judgement.'

'It's complicated,' she said, hearing the repetition of it, the weight of it bearing down on her like the promised storm.

The whole house seemed to shake with the knocking on the door.

'What is that, a neighbour?' Corey asked once she'd recovered herself.

Layne was looking at her, eyes wide, pondering her jumpy mother.

'I'll go,' Ruby said.

'Should you? I mean, no one's meant to be out, right? Nagin said—'

'Fuck Nagin. Someone might need our help.'

'I'm coming too.'

They went to the door, Corey holding back, Layne tucked behind her legs.

Ruby paused, a hand on the knob. 'We really need a peep hole.'

The door shuddered again and she started.

'Shit.' Ruby opened the door a crack, and swore again, and turned, saying, 'Ree, it's for you.' And as she swung the door wide open to reveal the two figures there, one in a hat supporting one in a hoodie, she said, 'It's your po'boy.'

<hr>

'I didn't think you'd still be here, not after the evac order,' Victor said, sipping coffee at the kitchen table.

Ruby stood by the percolator where another batch burbled. She'd suggested she take Layne to another room, but Corey insisted she stay.

'You sure you won't have some?' she asked Charlie, who was leaning against a cupboard of her wife's family's crockery, a Starbucks mug with the Space Needle in pride of place.

'I'm fine,' he said.

'You look pretty beat.'

'Been a long drive, straight through, listening to the radio.' He shook his head. 'Doesn't sound good.'

'You ladies shouldn't be here,' Victor said, as though they hadn't spoken. 'You should've taken Layne the hell away as soon as the storm tracked this way.'

'Stop telling me what to do. Roo wasn't leaving her wife and

I wasn't leaving her. Case closed, Vic. Besides, you wanted me to come back to another shootout?'

She was still getting over the shock of the two of them, though it was dark now and the coffee was on its second pot, Victor at the table and Charlie standing there like he was on guard while Layne played at his feet with Mr Bear, who he'd rescued, like he'd never been shot in the chest. Maybe his heart wasn't as fragile as he'd made out.

She could feel herself being pulled again, some kind of iron filing in a high school science experiment, being yanked between two magnets.

'We should evacuate,' Victor said. 'Curfew be damned. Had a hell of a time getting in, that's for sure. All the freeways are closed to inbound, they're not much better than a car park with everyone leaving. But we could try. Probably died down by now.'

'It's too late for that,' Ruby said. 'You don't wanna get caught out in the open. Like I told Ree, this house has stood the test. Safest place to be. We've got air mattresses and the couch, you can both sleep down here and we can work it out in the morning, once we see what Katrina does.'

The phone rang and she raced to the hallway to answer it, saying it would be Helena.

'I didn't expect to see the two of you, not together,' Corey said.

'Détente,' Victor said.

'While you make up your mind,' Charlie said.

'Is that fair?'

'Fairer than muskets at forty paces,' Victor said. 'For what good that's worth.'

Corey gripped her mug tight, fighting the urge to wring her hands clean off her wrists, to throw the mug at them, to run. But running, it seemed, was not a long-term solution. She hadn't been with Charlie long enough to master the art. The two of them were bloodhounds, anyway. Finding people was what they did. Knowing what to do with them once they'd found them, well, that was the question. How could she possibly make any decisions, here and now, when the storm was about to hit the city?

'You don't have to decide this minute,' Victor said, cutting off Charlie, who'd been saying much the same thing.

'Let's get through the storm first,' Charlie said. 'I'll go help with the bedding, once she's off the phone.'

'I'll do it, Charlie,' Corey said. 'You stay with Layne. She's missed you. Maybe you and Vic can keep her entertained, take her mind off things.' She paused at the door as Charlie scooped the kid up, promising her a piggyback to the living room to see what games Aunty Ruby has. Victor looked daggers but got up to follow them.

'Why do I have to choose?' she said. 'Why can't I have both?'

'Both?' Victor said.

Charlie cocked his head, his arms around the kid.

'Why not? Mormons do it. Muslims, I think.'

'That's the men,' Victor said.

'So?'

'I'm not the sharing kind.'

'Well, I have a kid, Vic. Sharing's part of the parcel.'

'That's different. She's my daughter.'

'She's Charlie's too.'

'I don't think Layne needs to hear this,' Charlie said. 'But for my money, it might have legs.'

'Jesus, are you serious? You'd be happy to have Corey and me … and you, at the same time?'

'I love her. I want her to be happy. And I have to accept there are things I cannot do … cannot be … for her. If she finds those things in you, who am I to stop her from having them? As long as I know she loves me, that she and Layne will be in my life, then, well, maybe it's worth thinking about.'

Corey kissed his cheek. 'This is why I love you, Charlie. It could be a way for us to get back what we had. I mean, I know you have needs, very real needs, that I can't fill up any more.'

'I was feeling you slip away, could feel the time in between us like a wedge. When you left, it broke me, Corey. But I know

I can't chain you to me, any more than you can chain me to you. That's not love, that's slavery. As long as we are honest and care for each other, respect each other, then I'll do anything to have you by my side. When you're with me, I don't need anything else.'

'Let me get this straight,' Victor said, standing, fists on the table. 'You want me to share you with a … with him? So how do you think that's gonna work exactly?'

'I don't know,' she said. 'We'll figure it out. But if you want to be in Layne's life, both of you, it's what we need to work out. I love you both, in my own way, and I don't see why I should have to give up either of you just because of convention. Fuck that.'

Victor shook his head. She could see him grappling with the concept, trying to see the future through the timber of the table in front of him. Imagining saying goodbye to her as she and Layne went off to be with Charlie, day shift/night shift. She almost laughed at the thought, but this was too serious. The air in the room had gone thick, as thick as the humidity in New Orleans in summer, and she was fighting for breath and covered in sweat as she watched – felt – the two men she cared for battle with their preconceptions and their egos and their needs and wants. Charlie wasn't like other men in so many ways, but he was still a man struggling to move with the times. But his blood trade had taught him to distance flesh from feelings; he'd suspected if not known she'd been sleeping with someone since the get-go and he hadn't minded, or so she thought, until it looked as if it might endanger their relationship and his relationship with Layne.

And Victor, Victor was all man, in the best and the worst ways, caring but so overprotective. He threatened Charlie's sense of security because he was so much that Charlie wasn't, could do so much that Charlie couldn't. Hell, all Victor had to do was step outside on a sunshiny day and Charlie couldn't touch him. Poor non-drinking, non-eating Charlie.

Ruby came in. 'Everyone still alive, I see. Excellent. We need to shore the house up, cover the windows. Helena says the storm's coming and it's gonna be a doozy.'

---

They ended up dragging the mattresses from the upstairs bedrooms down to the living room so they could all sleep in the one room. They'd dragged furniture against the windows and filled the basins and the bath.

'I hope the car will be all right,' Victor said.

'The car's the least of our worries,' Corey said.

Charlie seemed restless, like a dog on a chain, cooped up in the house as he stalked from window to window, and his restlessness grew with the wind.

She woke up in the night to the sound of rain smashing against the roof and windows and when she got up to look, it was as if someone were spraying a high-pressure hose again the pane. She couldn't see anything at all, just the water blasting against the glass. She cuddled her daughter, glad of Ruby and the solid form of Victor breathing deeply beside her, and the soft tread of Charlie, like a watchdog, prowling the space as though the storm were an intruder prying at their defences. Which, she figured, it was, but Ruby wasn't worried, only for her wife, at the hospital for who knew how long.

The storm's fury hit around 6am, tearing like a banshee, the wind incredible, deafening, like being inside a jet engine, the whole house shaking, and the sound of glass breaking and things tearing free, but thankfully nothing much on their place, repaying Ruby's confidence. She couldn't see much outside in the early-morning murk, the rain making the world grey and tossed through the glass. She marvelled at trees bent beyond breaking point, at signs and pieces of roof and metal being hurled through the air, and felt ridiculously glad to have the two men there, so stoic and solid as they distracted Layne.

Ruby went to make coffee but the power was out, and the radio was down to one station, callers from the coast saying whole towns were blown away. She pulled out a camp cooker to heat water so they could at least huddle with instant coffee.

'Guys,' Charlie said after maybe an hour or two, 'I think we need to move upstairs.'

Water was coming under the doors.

'Grab the mattresses,' Victor shouted.

They started hauling them back upstairs while Ruby threw down towels to try to stem the flow, then went to find a mop and bucket. 'The doors are, like, vibrating!' her muffled voice came from the kitchen.

'There's a leak somewhere, too,' Charlie said. 'I can hear it.'

'How can you hear anything?' Victor shouted.

They were still grappling with the last mattress when Layne pushed past, crying out for her bear. The toddler was quick and she made the living room before even Charlie could lay a hand on her.

'Come back, honey,' Corey called. 'We're going to camp upstairs.'

The back door burst open, like a SWAT team on steroids had just sunk the boot into it, and dirty water surged through, and the wind howled through the gap. Layne was caught in the stream and knocked off her feet. Charlie jumped down and by the time he had the child, was up to his knees. The whole house lurched as an almighty crash echoed through it, like a ship ramming a wharf. Charlie lost his footing and the two of them went down. Victor scrambled over the mattress as Corey screamed for Layne.

Victor was up to his waist in the water and barely able to push into the torrent swirling though the room. Branches whisked past, white bubbles catching torch light in the vicious eddies, as Charlie found his feet once more and was able to hoist Layne into Victor's arms. He had to lift her high to keep her from the water. Victor retreated up the stairs, the screaming child in his grip.

'Get upstairs, Corey. I've got her, she's safe.'

Layne was bawling, squirming.

'Where's Roo?' Corey shouted. 'Charlie, where's Ruby?'

He looked. Torch light shone greyly from the kitchen where she'd gone for the mop.

He forged that way, buffeted by two converging streams, one from the back deck and the other from the kitchen.

'Get upstairs,' Victor told Corey, but she shook her head.

'Not without Roo and Charlie.'

'It's filling up, Corey. We need to get higher.'

'There,' she said, pointing with the torch. 'He's got her.'

Charlie cradled Ruby in his arms, but her face was only just out of the water and covered by a dark splash. Charlie's eyes reflected red in the beam as he stumbled through the stormwater.

'Take Layne,' Victor said, passing the child to Corey, who fumbled with the torch, the beam going crazy around the room as she tried to hold the squirming child, Layne's screams adding to the din of the shredding wind.

Victor stepped down into the maelstrom, pushing past bobbing bits of household flotsam as he reached for Ruby. They got her to the stairs and Charlie managed to hand her over.

The house lurched again, a sudden shift that knocked the mattress into Corey. She dropped the torch. It bounced down and splashed into the water and swirled away, a glow quickly lost in the murk.

Victor shouted, 'I've got her, get upstairs, it's rising fast.'

Corey stumbled up, clutching her daughter, dragging her, as the inky flood chased her up the stairs. The house creaked like a boat trying desperately not to sink.

She made the hallway but she couldn't see where to go. There was a bedroom to the right, she knew, and the bathroom to the left with its sink and bath filled with water. She headed for that, to get towels, to get them dry and wash the filthy water from Layne, who reeked of mud.

Victor followed her and laid Ruby down.

'She's out. I think maybe a head knock. There's blood.'

Corey could barely see in the gloom. She washed Ruby's face and the dark stain flowed back from her forehead and across her closed eyes. Corey pressed a towel to her friend's face.

'There's a first-aid kit in the cupboard behind the mirror there,' she told Victor. 'She had it ready. I guess one benefit of living with a doctor.'

'If only the doctor was here,' Victor said as he rummaged around.

'There should be another torch, I think.'

He found it and they quickly assembled bandages and some antiseptic cream. At Corey's instruction, he got a pillow and blanket from the bedroom opposite, mercifully dry, and they made Ruby comfortable before getting Layne into dry clothes from Corey's room further down the hall.

'Where's Charlie?'

'He's … I don't know. I thought he was here. Like, behind me.'

'Oh, God. Stay with Layne. I'll be back.'

'Wait,' he shouted, but she was already moving. The stairway was filled with water. The flood was only two steps down and rising as she watched.

She ran back. 'I can't find him. The water … it's almost here.'

'Let's get on one of the beds, then.'

'I think maybe the attic.'

Ruby mumbled, groaned, rolled over and coughed.

'Roo, thank God.'

'I knew I needed an axe,' she mumbled.

'What?'

'On the radio. Before. They said to have an axe in the attic. In case you needed to chop your way out.'

'I'll chew our way out if I have to,' Victor said. 'We aren't dying here. I promise you.'

He pulled out his Nokia, its screen a dull glow. 'Nothing,' he said. 'Wouldn't it be neat if these things had torches built in?'

'Might as well ask for a lighter while you're at it,' Corey said.

'Help me up,' Ruby said. 'I'll show you the attic door.' She tweaked Layne's cheek. 'Ready for an adventure, kid? There's all kinds of treasure in the attic.'

She nodded but clung to Ruby while they pulled the ladder

down and collected what they could: clothes and blankets and the first-aid kit and a water bottle Corey had had beside her bed. By the time they were ensconced in the attic, the water was ankle-deep in the hallway and the storm was still screaming against the roof and there was no sign of Charlie.

'A bullet didn't stop him,' Victor said.

'No,' Corey said, aware of Ruby's quizzical glance as she set herself down gingerly beside her. 'But running water might.'

---

They sat in a circle around the radio. Victor kept an eye on the water level, but the house didn't seem to take any further damage. Judging by the reports on the radio, the same could not be said for New Orleans.

'They're saying the levees have broken.' Ruby's eyes turned to the back wall and the London Canal just beyond their fence.

'We're all right,' Victor said. 'I think that's the worst of it. Listen.'

It did seem the wind had dropped, and the darkness was lighter through the small attic window, and eventually the rain moved off.

'When I can, I should go offer my service,' Victor said. 'I'm sure they can use everybody they can get.'

'We should get to Mercy,' Ruby said.

'The Superdome's a shelter,' Corey said. 'But we should stay together. What if it comes back?'

'They're saying it's gone inland, it's petering out, but lots of flooding, and not just here,' Ruby said. 'There are people calling in to the radio, people in Biloxi caught like us in their attics. There are people on roofs. It's horrible.'

'Well, we can't do anything till the water goes down,' Victor said. 'Not unless you got a boat up here. Might as well take stock of our supplies and get comfortable. It might be a long wait.'

There came a thumping on the roof, and then a tearing sound as tiles were torn off. Sunlight spilled through a gap, and then a body fell through, head and shoulders first, flopping to the floor and dragging itself towards the nearest shadow.

'Oh my god, Charlie,' Corey said, as Layne ran over, arms outstretched, to cuddle him.

'Well, I'll be,' Victor said. 'I guess that answers the question about running water.'

# EPILOGUE

## 2009: SEATTLE

He awakes, daylight outlining the shutters of the shallow windows high on the wall. He makes his way to the stairs, past the guitars and the computers, and into the house.

From the living room window, he can see across the neighbour's roof to Maury Island, but his attention is on the backyard as he parts the curtain with a careful hand. They're pushing the kid on the swing though she's more than capable of doing it herself, the skirt of her school uniform ballooning around her. Victor has a beer in his hand. Corey is in a sun hat that covers her hair; he barely recognises her in her dress, although the shape of her silhouette through the black cotton is unmistakable. It's as though he doesn't exist, and it burns worse than the sun.

Regrets? He could've held Victor under, back there during Katrina. He could, just as easily, have used the storm to cover his retreat. Disaster was what Roy called a happy hunting ground, and given the magnitude of it, well, he could've lived on road kill quite well. No one would've noticed, especially if the bodies were black. Another storm victim wouldn't have rated a second glance, especially with Rita so close behind.

But he had done neither, caring too much for Corey to do the first and too much for himself to do the second.

So here they were, Corey rocking her grunge-goth writer career, Victor the doting detective partner, Layne somehow showing all the signs of being a well-adjusted kid with a huge imagination. Not bad given she kept a second, monstrous father in the basement.

Oh, he could venture out there, he supposes, some circus freak stumbling around in the daylight until his joints ache and his skin flares and cracks and his eyes bleed.

Corey looks up and he lets the curtain go. A few heartbeats and he hears her steps on the patio, then the door opening. He leans away from the sudden shaft of light. Every time, he wonders if this is the day she has decided to roll the dice. If she's hit the magic age to try to cross over from daytime to nighttime. Every time, no. This time is no different.

He smiles, unsure if he is disappointed or relieved.

'Hey sleepyhead,' she says, her voice husky.

He nods, taking in the lines around her eyes, her mouth, her throat.

'Thirsty?'

He smiles. 'Always.'

She jerks her head towards the door to his room in the basement.

And he can't resist, the hat thrown to the sofa, her fingers already undoing the buttons.

# ABOUT THE AUTHOR

Jason Nahrung grew up on a Queensland cattle property and now lives in Ballarat with his wife, the writer Kirstyn McDermott. He worked as a newspaper journalist for 30 years and runs a freelance editing practice. His fiction is anchored in the speculative genres and is invariably darkly themed, perhaps reflecting his passion for classic B-grade horror films and '80s goth rock. He is the author of four novels – all involving vampires in an Australian setting — and more than 20 short stories. He also has a strong interest in climate fiction, which led him to complete a PhD in creative writing from The University of Queensland. Find him online at www.jasonnahrung.com.

THANK YOU FOR BUYING THIS
BRAIN JAR PRESS BOOK

To receive special offers, bonus content, and info on
new releases and other great reads, visit us
online at www.BrainJarPress.com

9 781922 479662